D1404260

Hollywood
&Maine

allison whittenberg

Hollywood
&Maine

DELACORTE PRESS

Published by Delacorte Press
an imprint of Random House Children's Books
a division of Random House, Inc.
New York

Delacorte Press and colophon are registered trademarks of
Random House, Inc.

Visit us on the Web! www.randomhouse.com/kids

Educators and librarians, for a variety of teaching tools,
visit us at www.randomhouse.com/teachers

Library of Congress Cataloging-in-Publication Data
Whittenberg, Allison.
Hollywood and Maine / Allison Whittenberg. — 1st ed.
p. cm.
Summary: In 1976 Pennsylvania, middle-schooler Charmaine Upshaw
contemplates a career as a model or actress while coping with
boyfriend problems and the return of her uncle, a fugitive who
cost her family $1,000 in bail money a year earlier.
ISBN 978-0-385-73671-8 (trade)—ISBN 978-0-385-90623-4 (library)
ISBN 978-0-375-89203-5 (e-book)
[1. Family life—Pennsylvania—Fiction. 2. African Americans—Fiction.
3. Interpersonal relations—Fiction. 4. Middle schools—Fiction. 5. Schools—Fiction.
6. Pennsylvania—History—20th century—Fiction.] I. Title.
PZ7.W6179Hol 2009
[Fic]—dc22
2008035679

The text of this book is set in 12-point Goudy.

Book design by Kenny Holcomb

Printed in the United States of America

10 9 8 7 6 5 4 3 2 1

First Edition

This book is dedicated and in memoriam to
Luther Whittenberg (my daddy).
Thanks for being the music of the house.
I take your songs with me always.

one

A bicentennial is one hundred times two. Two hundred years, that's how long there had been a nation known as the United States of America, and there I, Charmaine Upshaw, was, fortunate enough to be living in the birthplace of it all, Philadelphia, Pennsylvania.... Yawn.

It was the second week of January 1976, and already I was sick of seeing those colors: red, white, and blue. Three colors I liked separately but that looked a little lame when thrown together. (This was the one time I was thankful that my family only had a black-and-white TV set.) Even so, I was assaulted by that endless fifing and drum beating during commercial breaks.

Though I wasn't riveted by the public celebration, luckily I had a private milestone to mark. Finally, and I do mean fi-nal-ly, I had a real boyfriend. This was progress, because last term, I'd only had a fake one. Not just any fake boyfriend—I'd had a gorgeous fake boyfriend. His name was Demetrius McGee, and he did to me what dogs do to fire hydrants. But that was all through now. Although few would have described my new beau as a dreamboat, Raymond Newell was definitely an improvement.

Tonight, he was coming over for his first dinner with my family. I was abuzz, endlessly patting my 'fro and running a lint brush over my blouse. In the background, I listened to the best singer in the world: Al Green. As he hit those high highs and those low lows, I thought of another thing I could celebrate. I was grateful to have my own stereo in my own room. I had inherited both from my older brother, who had just been stationed in Hawaii. I dabbed perfume behind my ears and glanced over at the clock. It was nearly five. I wondered where the last hour had gone as I quickly but neatly folded the clothes I had taken out and put them back in the closet.

After making one more adjustment to my top and dusting off my jeans, I tore downstairs.

To my horror, my other brother, Leo, and my cousin Tracy John had just begun a jigsaw puzzle. Most of the 120 pieces were scattered across the living room floor.

"Will you get all this mess out of the way?" I asked them.

Tracy John looked around, playing dumb. "Is she talking to us?"

I marched into the kitchen. Before I had a chance to

launch my complaint, Ma turned from the stove and said, "I thought you were putting on a skirt."

"I don't want to wear a skirt, Ma."

"It would look much better." She had antiquated girls-shouldn't-wear-dungarees values and an Alabama accent. She turned back to what she was cooking.

I put my hands on my hips. "Leo and Tracy John have that puzzle spread all across the place. Raymond is going to think we live in a pigpen."

"Take your hands off your imagination."

"Are you going to say anything to them?" I asked.

"Boys, please put your game away," she called over her shoulder.

"Yes, ma'am," they said in unison.

Ma looked back at me and said, "All you had to do was ask."

I took a whiff of what was cooking and went closer to the oven. I opened it to find an arrangement of pork chops oozing with juiciness.

"Dammit!" I exclaimed.

"This kitchen is no place for cussing," Ma told me.

I shook my head. "Ma, Raymond can't eat this!"

The boys entered the kitchen.

"Why, doesn't Spider-Man like chops?" Tracy John asked.

"He would like to be referred to as Raymond," I said.

"He can't change his nickname this late," Leo said. "Everybody at school knows him as Spider-Man."

"People have a right to be called what they want to be called," Ma said.

"Is he going to break out if he eats a pork chop?" Leo asked.

My hands fluttered up to my temples. "Raymond's not allergic to pork chops. It's just that he's a—"

"Maybe if you didn't waste the last hour trying on different outfits, Charmaine, you'd know what I was putting on the table." Ma cut me off as she hurried past me with the place settings.

"Yeah, and that getup looks the same as the one you first had on," Leo said.

I followed behind Ma, adjusting the salt and pepper shakers on the table. "Maybe you can whip up something else, please?"

Ma raised one hand in graceful protest. "I'm not a short-order cook."

I threw my shoulders back, went into the kitchen, and opened the fridge. "Then I'll make him something."

"Close that icebox, Charmaine."

"Ma, he doesn't eat pork."

She came behind me and closed the refrigerator door. "Then tell him it's chicken."

Just then, the doorbell rang. My heart raced with excitement.

I opened it to find my beau in a dress shirt, tie, and pressed slacks, with a wide smile on his face. My eyes got wistful for a moment.

"Hello, Maine," he said.

"Hello, Raymond," I said.

"Hi, Spider-Man," Tracy John said.

I hadn't noticed that he'd run up behind me. I turned to my cousin. "What did I just say he wanted to be called?"

"That's all right. Tracy John can call me whatever he wants."

"Don't open that door," Leo yelled out from the kitchen.

"Hi, Leo," Raymond yelled back.

Tracy John pointed to the tall bottle Raymond held. "Is that booze?"

Now I laughed a little. "Of course not," I said. But to Raymond I whispered, "Is it?"

Raymond told us it was sparkling cider.

Ma came into the room, wiping her hands on her apron. "You didn't have to bring anything."

"It's my pleasure, Mrs. Upshaw."

Ma broke into a smile that was shy and girlish.

We gathered in the living room to kill some time before supper, and Ma immediately asked about Raymond's parents. Raymond filled her in with basically what I'd told her before. His folks worked in the Philadelphia school district as principals.

"There are schools with two principals?" Leo asked.

I gritted my teeth. "Not at the same school."

"Are they nice principals or mean ones?" Tracy John asked.

Raymond grinned. "Remember, your principal is your pal."

5

I saw Tracy John mulling that over before he said, "No he's not."

The grin still hadn't left Raymond's face.

"Raymond is an only child," I told them.

Ma nodded. "That explains your patience."

"So what made you want to go out with Maine?" Leo asked.

I rolled my eyes heavenward, seeking strength. Real subtle, Leo.

"I have been admiring her from afar for quite a while. Ever since I first laid eyes on her in seventh-grade art class."

"Two years ago!" Leo exclaimed. "It took you that long?"

"I had to muster my courage," Raymond proclaimed. "Profound, utter beauty can be a frightening thing. It can paralyze you and leave you tongue-tied."

Confusion swept over Tracy John's face, and he asked Leo, "Is he still talking about Maine?"

Raymond laughed warmly and continued, "This little lady here has such physical charms that I even entered her in a contest."

"A beauty contest?" Leo asked.

"Kind of," Raymond said. "A modeling contest."

"A model in a magazine?" Tracy John asked.

"No, on a spaceship," I said.

"What did it cost to enter this contest?" Leo asked.

"Just postage for the letter," Raymond said.

Leo snickered. "Well, I guess that's worth fifteen cents."

I frowned and looked over to my mother, who said, "It never hurts to try."

Another ringing endorsement, I thought.

"Not only does Charmaine possess looks, but also poise and grace."

Feeling as if I was about to drown in this syrup, I said, "Raymond, stop."

"Yes, please stop," Leo said.

Raymond pushed me playfully. "Not only is she attractive, but she's so smart. She's a walking encyclopedia."

I gave him a gentle shove back. "No, you are."

"No, you are." He winked and shoved me once again.

"No, you—"

"Oh, call it a draw." Tracy John jumped in.

Good-natured still, Raymond opened the bottle. Ma had already set out the glasses for the five of us, and one for Daddy, who would be home any minute.

"A toast to Maine," Raymond called out.

Everyone raised a glass except Tracy John.

"I don't want that," he told us.

"What's wrong now?" I asked him.

"I don't know what that is." Tracy John spoke with great authority, as if at six years old he could be an expert in anything.

"It's like apple juice," I said.

"Why does it have bubbles?" Tracy John asked, moving the glass away from him.

"It's like apple juice and soda," I said.

He looked suspiciously at the glass. Ma fawned over

him, asking, "Don't you want to try just a teensy-weensy little bit, sweetheart?" till finally he tried a sip.

I could tell he was glad he did, because he gulped some more, then commented, "This ain't half bad, Spider-Man."

We said "Cheers," and at the moment when our glasses met in the air, I heard the back door unlatch. Daddy came in and swept the room once over with his pine-bark brown eyes. He asked, "Y'all drinking this early?"

After grace, it was a countdown to when the fireworks would start. Ma offered Raymond first pick from the pork chops.

"No, thank you, Mrs. Upshaw," Raymond said. "I'm a vegetarian."

"Maine told us you were Catholic," Leo said.

Ma held the server; she was kind of frozen. "Is that what you were trying to tell me, Charmaine?"

"In so many words," I said.

"I'm sorry, Mrs. Upshaw. I don't eat meat."

"Never, Raymond?" Ma asked him.

"You've never had a hamburger?" Tracy John was more forceful in his questioning.

Raymond shook his head.

"How about a hamburger bun?" Leo asked.

But before Raymond had a chance to answer, Daddy asked, "Well, how about some fish?" He tried to rescue Ma by passing the server around in the other direction, then said, "Miss Sweet Thang, we got any of that fried flounder from last night left in the icebox? You ain't got nothing against leftovers, Raymond, do you?"

"I'm sorry, Mr. Upshaw. I don't eat fish either."

Daddy's eyebrows shot up higher.

Stealthily, I pushed the breadbasket Raymond's way.

"The boy can't make a meal off of rolls," Daddy told me.

Raymond added the sides to his plate to make it look full. He ate a forkful of vegetables and said, "Mmmm, Mr. Upshaw, this is just fine."

"Well, why don't we all dig in," Daddy said, and set the example by knifing into the chop that lay before him.

Tracy John, whose eyes were fixed on Raymond, didn't make a move toward his meal.

Raymond continued to smile pleasantly, and after a while Tracy John started eating as instructed.

"Tell me, Raymond, what do you like to do in your free time?" Ma asked.

"I like to listen to music, Mrs. Upshaw."

"Oh, isn't that nice. Who do you like to listen to?"

"I like Marian Anderson."

"Is she in the Fifth Dimension?" Leo asked.

I dropped my fork. "That's Marilyn McCoo. Marian Anderson is a famous opera singer."

"Opera," Daddy repeated. He held up his hands. "That's too much doggone culture for me."

"What's opera?" Tracy John asked.

"It's like the music they play on *Bugs Bunny*," Leo said.

"That Marian Anderson grew up around here. She was a South Philly girl," Daddy said.

"And now she belongs to the world," I said.

"Oh, the gowns. The wonderful sequined gowns she wears," Ma said.

"That woman must be seven feet tall," Daddy said.

"Is that taller than you, Maine?" Tracy John asked me. Leo laughed loudly.

Raymond turned to Leo and said, "Maine tells me you are a talented dancer."

I watched a smirk grow on my brother's face. What a way to take a compliment! Puffing up like an ostrich.

Raymond turned to Tracy John. "And she also tells me that you are a peewee-league football player."

A mournful look swept across Tracy John's face. "Not no more, the season just ended."

"What's up next for you?" Raymond asked.

I should have warned Raymond beforehand. This was a sore subject with Tracy John. "Tracy John is a little disappointed because baseball starts soon."

"Yeah, because baseball's boring," Tracy John told Raymond.

Daddy pointed at Tracy John with his fork. "Now, what did I tell you about thinking like that? We had to fight like heck to get into the majors."

"Blacks were in the football league before the baseball league, Daddy?" Leo asked.

"Years before," Daddy said. "The NFL was integrated before World War Two."

Another round of rolls was passed.

"Well, if that's true," I said, "how come they always say Jackie Robinson broke the color line in sports? Even before baseball, didn't that runner in the 1936 Olympics break the barrier?"

"Jesse Owens," Raymond said.

I squeezed his hand. "That's him."

"That was in Germany," Daddy said. "And that was more of an event type of thing. Baseball happens every year and the season is longer than football."

"All right then, how about that boxer—"

"Jack Johnson?" Raymond guessed.

I shook my head. "No. Not him."

"You're talking about Joe Louis," Daddy said.

I nodded.

"The Brown Bomber held the heavyweight title ten years before number forty-two took the field," Raymond said.

Leo agreed. "Football, track, and boxing are more exciting than baseball."

"Maybe so, but they ain't called America's favorite pastime," Daddy said.

Tracy John leaned on his elbows. "America's favorite *boring* pastime."

"Now, now, Tracy John, let's not be a wet blanket," Daddy told him.

But really, it wasn't until Ma brought out a red velvet cake that brooding Tracy John perked back up.

After dinner, the gathering dispersed into twos. Leo and Tracy John went their way. Daddy and Ma went another. Raymond and I retired to the living room, and we spent the next hour or so talking and looking longingly into each other's eyes. When it came time for Raymond to leave, we dipped into the kitchen so he could say good night properly. We came to find that Raymond's "odd ways" were still the topic at hand.

Daddy gestured wildly. "Have you ever heard of anything like that, Miss Sweet Thang? No meat ever? As bony as that boy is?"

Ma shrugged. "Peyton, he seems like a well-mannered young man."

"Lord have mercy. And then he even turned down the fish I offered him. I thought Catholics ate fish. But maybe that's only on Fridays." Daddy got to the end of his sentence before he noticed us by the entrance of the room.

Raymond came forward to shake Daddy's hand. "Thanks so much for your hospitality. Everything was wonderful."

As I walked him to the front door, Raymond did more than his share of smiling, waving, and thanking as my family quickly assembled in the hallway. They swarmed like buzzards.

Before departing, Raymond took my hand, turned it

palm side up, and gave it a wet, passionate kiss right there on the inside.

Then he let me go and reached for the doorknob, and he was gone.

Daddy, Ma, Leo, and Tracy John weren't discreet about their gawking; their four pairs of eyes were just as wide.

Daddy let out a deep-throated chuckle and said, "Charmaine, looks like you have got yourself a real Romeo."

two

"How does he do it?" Millicent, my best friend, asked the next day at lunch.

"Here, I'll show you." I took her hand in mine and closed my eyes like Raymond had done and nosed into her palm, leaving a kiss there.

"I don't get it," Cissy, my other best friend, said.

"He did that right in front of your parents?" Millicent asked.

"It's just on the hand," I said.

"I hope you're not pregnant," Millicent said.

"Very funny," I said, and sipped on my carton of grape juice. I was the first from our trio to have a boyfriend, so I was used to this ribbing. It was a toss-up who would be next. Would it be Millicent, with her fuzzy French braids and talkative manner, or Cissy, with her full figure and cute laugh? Though Dardon Junior High wasn't exactly overflowing with hot prospects, I didn't think it would take much longer for either one of them. I suspected that very soon they would be walking in my moccasins, and I would have the pleasure of giving them the third degree.

Cissy took another bite of the square school pizza she'd been eating. She was more daring than I. That dried-out yellow-brown cheese frightened me.

Millicent resumed her questioning. "What did your parents think of him?"

"Well, Ma said Raymond is very well-mannered."

"Like a dog?" Cissy asked.

"That's well-behaved," I said.

"How do you like him?" Millicent asked.

"Of course I like him. We've been going out since Kwanzaa."

"No, Maine," Cissy said, then added, with great inflection, "Do you *really* like him?"

"Yeah, do you think you have a future together?" Millicent asked.

So many questions . . . I mused over the idea of life with Raymond Newell and came up with "I don't know; we're both Virgos."

"Uh-oh, you need a Sagittarius," Millicent said.

"No, she needs a Gemini," Cissy disagreed.

"I think that's his rising sign," I said.

"Well, then it will probably work out," Millicent said with a bright smile.

———

After school I went to Raymond's house. He lived on Redwood Avenue. He took out the key and unlocked the door, and we crossed the threshold. His house wasn't much bigger than mine, but it had more gadgets. Raymond's house had a garbage disposal, a blender, and even a dishwasher. According to Ma, we had a dishwasher too. It was called Charmaine.

Raymond wasn't the only only child I knew. Millicent was an only child also, but her grandmother lived with her and her parents, giving their home that full old-people smell. In Raymond's house, there was a lot of space. Space that felt like emptiness, making me want to shout to hear my echo.

We went upstairs to his room, replete with his personal color TV and a private telephone, and I was back to thinking that he was living the life. He had normal albums like Stevie Wonder and Marvin Gaye, but he also had opera albums for his private edification.

I flipped through the covers to find Marian Anderson near the top.

Raymond stopped me, saying, "We don't have to listen to that, Maine. You said your favorite was Al Green."

He placed his record on the turntable and Green's hit "Let's Stay Together" started to play. As we listened, Raymond held my hands and told me how pretty they were. I brought up how he kissed me last night.

"You know where I got that from?" he asked.

I shook my head.

"Rudolf Valentino. He starred in *The Sheik*."

"Was he an Arab?" I asked.

"No, Italian."

"Oh, right, Valentino."

"He was known as the Latin Lover."

I looked about the room. There were posters up and memorabilia of Hollywood's bygone era. He pulled out an oversized book and turned to near the end. "It's alphabetized," he explained. "Here he is."

I surveyed the pictures. This Valentino definitely had a dashing profile. He had a turban on his head in one photo. In another, he was kissing a woman's palm.

"Where are my manners?" Raymond asked. "Can I get you something to drink?"

"Sure," I said. I was expecting more of the bubbly sparkling cider.

"I'll make us some cocoa," he promised.

Even better, I thought, and smiled as he left the room.

I moved to the middle of the book. The top of the page told me that this was the one and only Marilyn Monroe. It was a name I'd heard, but I never really took the time to look at her face. She had a real innocent, surprised expression, like a newborn fawn. The passage on her was full of tidbits, like that she came into this world wrapped in the hideously plain name of Norma Jean Mortenson.

Another fact I uncovered, and this one was startling: She was a trained actress. It said she studied at the Actors

Studio with Lee Strasberg, which sounded important and respectable.

As I read on, I was stunned to find that that pretty face with that pretty smile hadn't led a very pretty life.

She had a father who didn't recognize her as his daughter, and a mother who was placed in a mental institution. All throughout Marilyn's childhood, she bounced around in foster care. In adulthood, though she found fame and fortune, she still wasn't able to locate good luck. She had a number of divorces and miscarriages. To top it off, Marilyn Monroe was known to mix champagne with sleeping pills. I found it hard to believe that with all the people she had clamoring around her on a movie set, not a single soul had the sense to pull her aside and set her straight. If only I'd been there, she would have definitely heard my thoughts on the matter. If it's one thing I'm not, it's shy.

I continued to page through the text and found a piece about someone named Elizabeth Taylor (who, it said, had violet eyes, though I don't think that's humanly possible), and another one about someone named Marlene Dietrich (who had killer bone structure; it said she had her back teeth removed to create such hollows).

Within the five minutes I'd been left with the book, I began to tire of Hollywood. It was one white face after another, all variations on the same Eurocentric theme. Then I stumbled upon her, and I found myself thinking something I never thought I would: Thank God for

Dorothy Dandridge. If it hadn't been for her, we would have been shut out of this 500-plus-page monstrosity.

The passage stated that Dandridge was the first (and only) black actress ever to be nominated for Best Actress, and that doggone flaxen-haired Grace Kelly had to go and beat her out for the award. What did Kelly need with an Academy Award, anyway? She was already part of society. Her family was the very definition of Old Philadelphia wealth. In addition to that, Kelly retired from acting shortly after she received the Oscar and moved to Monaco and became a princess.

After her loss, Dandridge took a nosedive, sinking into obscurity, bankruptcy, and an untimely death. I had never looked at things from this perspective, but next to Grace Kelly's regal blond flawlessness, it dawned on me that raven-haired Dorothy Dandridge did look downright, dare I say, exotic.

Raymond came back with two steaming cups. He handed one to me. One sip told me: This wasn't cocoa. This was that horrible Ovaltine. It didn't taste like chocolate; it tasted like medication.

"I didn't put too much in, did I?" he asked.

I suppressed my wince. "No, it's just perfect."

I studied his expression as he drank. Did he really like Ovaltine? Or was he like everyone else, pretending?

"So how do you like the book, Maine?"

I shrugged.

"Were you reading about Valentino?"

"I skipped around. I read a lot about Marilyn Monroe."

"She had that real charisma, didn't she? You can borrow it, if you'd like. You could read about the rest."

"No thanks," I said, putting the book down. "There's not enough of us in here."

"Us?"

"Yeah, people who look like you and me."

"Well, as your dad was saying about baseball last night, we have had a hard time getting into motion pictures, too," Raymond said.

"But there was never a ban on blacks being in movies."

"No, there was nothing official. Unfortunately, even now, we just don't seem to get a lot of glamorous parts," Raymond said. "And that's really unfortunate, because, Maine, you're prettier than any girl in this book."

I waved him away. "Oh, come on."

"Maine." His face broke into a free smile. "You should borrow the book. You are Marilyn Monroe with an Afro."

When you wear glasses, there's no such thing as spontaneity. I found that it helped greatly to take them off before I moved in too close.

I used to be turned off by Raymond because he was built like me, gangly. I always pictured myself with someone more substantial. And since most people thought of me as an egghead, I had visions of myself with someone who took the world less seriously.

But Raymond worked on me, especially during moments like this.

I'd gotten used to his somewhat protruding eyelids,

which, before, I'd thought were toad-froggish. Now I liked his peepers. Even his wide smile reminded me of a friendly alligator.

With my glasses off, all his features collapsed into a haze anyway.

We touched lips, and it was magic.

three

I walked home with Raymond's book, lifted by his compliment and the kiss, but my balloon of contentment was quickly punctured.

Ma met me at the entrance to the kitchen with this question: "Did you ask before you went over that boy's house?"

"Last night, you said he had manners."

"That was while he was here. Chaperoned. You told me both his parents work. Who was there to oversee you two?"

I looked beyond her to see what was for supper. Crawfish were laid out by the sink. Pleading the fifth, I walked past her and began to devein them. After I removed the heads from the shells, I stripped out the crap. I hoped that Ma would move on to other lines of questioning, but she was like a dog with a bone. She just wouldn't let go.

"Was the light on?"

"It was daylight, Ma."

"Did you turn out the lights?"

"I just looked at his Hollywood books," I reassured her.

That seemed to agitate her more. "You looked at his what, now?"

"He has books on movie stars."

"What's that, some kind of code?" she asked.

Parents are such hypocrites. Ma never passed up an opportunity to counsel me on the value of chastity despite the fact that she was not much older than me when she took off with a sailor. Oh, yes she did. I guess it was a thunderbolt because Daddy, who was only about twenty, was on shore leave when they met. What I'm trying to say is that it wasn't like Ma's parents knew him all that well before Ma identified him as the one she was about to marry. What I wouldn't give to be a fly on the wall during that unveiling!

Daddy, aka Petty Officer First Class Peyton Upshaw, got an honorable discharge after he completed his initial enlistment contract and said goodbye to a life on the sea. He moved his (very) young bride and child back to his hometown, West Philly. That was the first time they had actually lived together as a family. My older brother, Horace, was nearly three, and I guess things went well because I came along later that year and then Leo the following year.

I followed Ma into the living room and asked, "Who's the extra place for?"

"Your uncle E."

I thought for a minute, then shrugged. I had two uncles, and I was sure she had misspoken. "You mean Uncle O is coming over?"

"I mean what I said. Uncle E is coming over."

Her delivery was so flat that the gravity of the situation took a while to really set in, and when it did, the words *Uncle E* cut through me like a straight razor. For, you see, the earth is curved, the sun is hot, and Uncle E is the family deadbeat. I hadn't seen him since he skipped town, leaving us with a whopping one thousand in bail money forfeited to the court.

"He called early today," Ma said.

"He called!" I said, suddenly frayed thin. "He called on the phone?"

"Yes, he called on the phone. He said he hopes he can be here by dinner, but he might have to work late."

"He has a job?" I asked.

"Apparently so, Charmaine."

"Maine, did you hear the news?" Tracy John asked, running up beside me.

I nodded. It was the equivalent of sticking a butter knife in a toaster—I was shocked. Uncle E was coming over. Low-down-rotten-good-for-nothing Uncle E. I looked for a place to sit down and collect myself. Wasn't it supposed to be in the newspaper when big things happened, like hell freezing over?

So now he was back. This guy had a rap sheet that

would fill up a blackboard. It dated clear back to 1957. Now he was in town. For what, I could only wonder.

It was five, then six, and Uncle E still hadn't come. As dinner went from hot to room temperature to cool, I thought things had been going too well, what with finally having a boyfriend and all. I should have known something terrible was going to happen, like I'd be stricken with leprosy and lose a couple of fingers, or a plague of locusts would descend on eastern Pennsylvania.

Uncle E didn't make it by dinner, and we held out till nearly eight. Everyone seemed disappointed, but with every ticktock of the clock I heard, I felt more relieved. Maybe he wouldn't come over at all.

My luck ran out around nine. The doorbell rang and everyone (but me) rushed to the door. I took it slow. I observed him from afar and noted that he was pretty much as I remembered. He was Daddy's height, just under six feet. Uncle E was slimmer, whereas Daddy was more muscular. But Uncle E's eyes, which I recalled used to be so intense and jittery—an occupational hazard, I suppose—now seemed relieved, even calm.

He said to my cousin, "I know you, you're Karyn."

That wasn't exactly an original thought. Nearly everyone said that about Tracy John.

"He sure looks like her, don't he?" Ma said.

"Yeah, especially in the face," Uncle E said.

I rolled my eyes. What a dumb thing to say. Where else would Tracy John resemble his mother at—his feet?

"Hey, Leo!" he called out.

"Uncle E!" Leo called back. "We thought we'd never see you again."

"Well, he's here now," Ma said. "Welcome."

"Thank you, Lela Mae," Uncle E said to Ma. "Thank you deeply."

He next got to me. "And this must be Maine, looking so tall and grown."

Go *away!* I felt like saying but, of course, didn't. "Nice to see you again," I lied. Then I went back to sulking.

I noted that for once Uncle E was clean-shaven, and the scar on his left cheek wasn't as deep or wide as I remembered it. Also, there was a really fresh scent coming off him. What a con artist. I wish I could have told him that I was on to him. I wouldn't care if he'd just taken five baths in a row—as far as I was concerned, he'd never come clean.

It was a funny thing: With all this emotion swirling around the atmosphere of our living room, no one seemed to notice my scowl. Then it dawned on me: Daddy hadn't spoke up yet. Hope sprang anew. It might be worth it to see Daddy's reaction to his long-lost brother, Escalus.

This was the man who was nowhere to be found for months.

This was the man who made Daddy lose one thousand dollars.

This was the man who left Daddy stranded in that courthouse, waiting.

Let him have it, Daddy.

Daddy opened his arms wide to Escalus and said, "Oh, brother!"

Oh, brother was right.

I leaned against the molding, my arms crossed in further study. This was straight-up sickening. I've heard of turning the other cheek, but this was insane.

Suddenly, tears of elation streamed from my father's eyes.

Ma was well into *her* waterworks.

I took this opportunity to duck out. I couldn't take this farce one more second.

Washing dishes made such an ugly sound: *Slosh, slosh, slosh.* But at least it took up time. Time I didn't have to spend in the same room with Uncle E.

When Ma popped in I asked, "How long is he going to stay?"

"What a question! He is our guest. He can stay as long as he wants."

"Did he come with a check to reimburse us?"

"That's between your daddy and him."

"Oh, I'm sorry. I thought I was a resident of 614 Dardon Avenue."

"I know exactly of where you are a resident. I'm just telling you, Charmaine, this ain't your show."

She went back to the gathering. I peeked in and saw everyone carrying on a plain conversation as if Uncle E had never taken flight.

Daddy kept offering his brother food, a drink, and a seat.

Uncle E kept declining, saying he had to go because he had to wake up early the next morning.

How early? He said 4 a.m.

"I really just came by to see all of y'all," he said as he finally made a motion toward the door.

Daddy all but blocked his exit. "Well, you just can't say hi and bye after all this time."

He can't? I thought.

"Maybe I have time for one song," Uncle E said.

"Don't tell me you brought it?" Daddy asked.

"Brought what?" Tracy John asked.

"You'll see," Daddy promised.

Uncle E went outside and came back holding a six-stringed, light brown guitar by its neck.

Daddy started clapping. As if at a concert, all Uncle E had to do was take to the stage to gain applause. "Uppercase E, play that one song," Daddy requested.

"You mean—"

"Uh-huh," Daddy said.

My interest piqued, I stepped into the room. I wondered what that one song could be. "Jailhouse Rock" or "Chain Gang"?

Uncle E began with his eyes closed, and I recognized the song immediately. "Nobody Knows You When You're Down and Out."

At that blues song, I really began to fume. Let's get one thing straight, Escalus Upshaw, you left us high and dry, not the other way around. What revisionist history! He was spewing lines like "In your pocket, not one penny / And as for friends, you don't have any." He got the whole thing twisted. We never ditched him. He's the one who skipped town.

Uncle E really dragged out the lyrics about being high on the hog and then luck changing. He didn't have to tell me that things turned on a dime. Just a few hours earlier, I was happy to be called an Afroed Marilyn Monroe, now look at me.

The rest of my family was hypnotized. They were bobbing their heads along.

Silently, I admitted that Uncle E was nimble, with his fingers contorting to different positions and his tenor voice pitch-perfect. But I showed no outward approval.

When he ended the song, Daddy did the "Oh, yeah!"

Tracy John did the "Woohoo!"

Leo clapped.

Ma was tearing up fresh tears.

And me, well, I was kind of all by my lonesome. The momentum was too high. I was outnumbered; I couldn't make any difference. If I'd spoken up, I'd have been like a little dog yapping at the parade passing by. Because I hated to feel small, I clammed up and endured.

four

With its stained-glass windows and various Stations of the Cross, Raymond's church, Our Lady of the Rosary, was more decorated than my church, Friendship AME. With the service's pattern of kneel, stand, sit, and kneel some more, there was a rhythm to it. Despite all this movement, my visit was done and over in three quarters of an hour. Services at my church usually took half the day, and that was when Reverend Clee was keeping it brisk. That was another difference. Catholics called their reverends priests.

This priest was from the continent of Africa. I had heard that all major religions had been practiced in the motherland: Christianity, Judaism, and Islam. I wondered if this onyx-colored man at the pulpit was from one of those villages where the only way you were ever going to get schooling was to follow the mission.

Raymond told me there were millions of African

Catholics, which caused me to ponder: If there were those kinds of numbers, would there ever be a black pope?

I sat in the fourth row between Raymond and his parents, who both had hair as white as Elmer's glue. They had pleasant enough faces, but they appeared so old that Raymond could have been mistaken for their great-grandson. They were sedate and calm during the entire Mass, as it was called. Everyone was. There wasn't a "Yes, Lord" spoken, and nobody asked, "Can I get a witness?" I guessed this was largely due to the fact that the priest delivered his sermon completely in Latin.

"Do you know what he's saying?" I asked Raymond.

"No one does," Raymond replied.

I fought off a judgmental frown by setting my hopes on communion time. That was when I would get to take a swig of some of that wine.

That part was at the very end. I made my way up to the altar with the single-file line and found disappointment again. I knew grape juice when I tasted it.

That afternoon, I went home to face the music—literally. I expected to see Uncle E and hear more from his songbook. I peeked in a few rooms to find that he wasn't there. (There *is* a God.)

I passed Leo in the hallway. He told me, "Non-Catholics aren't supposed to go to *their* church. I hope you don't go to Hell for that, Maine."

"That's nothing to joke around about," I told him.

He skittered away, laughing.

As I walked into the kitchen, Ma up-and-downed me. "How was the service?"

"It was all right. Quick."

She nodded. "Did you have one of them cookies?"

"They are called communion wafers, Ma."

"Communion wafers," she repeated. "Are they sweet?"

"No."

"So you did have one."

"I wasn't supposed to. Raymond said you are supposed to be confirmed before you accept the sacrament."

A worried look swept across her face. "He said you have to be what to accept the what, now?"

"You didn't go AME till you met Daddy."

"Baptist and AME ain't that far apart."

"Neither is Catholic," I said.

She seemed like she wanted to say something but changed her mind and went back to fixing a side dish, which, by the looks of things, consisted of cracked rice cooked with crushed tomatoes and chopped-up sausage. She poured in a liberal amount of chicken broth. That's how dependent on meat the Upshaw family was; we even needed it to make rice.

I tried to ease my way out before she started dispersing chores on me.

"Charmaine, make a pitcher of lemonade, will you?" she requested.

I washed my hands and began mashing the lemons. When I was done mixing the juice with sugar, a little

32

ginger, and water, I took a taste test. I winced from the tartness, but since I was a little peeved at my family, I smiled. This was good enough for them.

"Maine, Maine. I'm glad you're back." Tracy John ran up to me and started tugging at my sleeve. Those penny-colored eyes of his were stretched wide. "I wanted to ask you about dinosaurs."

That statement made me smile because the urgency of his voice didn't match his subject matter.

"Remember when we read that book about dinosaurs?"

"Yes."

"You said they were all gone, but I saw on TV where this plane landed somewhere in this place where they was nothing but dinosaurs."

I took a step back and folded my arms. "What kind of show is that?"

"I don't know, but I saw it."

"That's just something made up," I reassured him.

"It looked real," he insisted.

"There is no way that could happen. Airplanes exist now, but all the dinosaurs died out millions of years ago."

"Then how come they showed it on TV?"

"Don't believe everything you see on television. Believe me, Tracy John: Dinosaurs are extinct."

"You stink," he said, and made his favorite fang-face at me. Then he left the room in a comic, highly orchestrated huff.

"Can you believe what he said to me?" I asked Leo as he entered the room.

Leo shrugged. "Have you tried Ban Roll-On?"

During baked chicken and red rice supper, I had to listen to more rave reviews of Uncle E.

Daddy was with the "What an interpretation!"

Ma was with the "My. My. My."

Leo did the "Where was he hiding all that talent?"

Tracy John just said "Yep" a lot.

I had a newsflash for all of them: Singing was something we are known for. Some even feel that it's in our genetic makeup, like the melanin in our skin. I didn't believe that such a thing could be passed on through DNA, but I did know one thing: There were plenty of black men with good voices.

"And his guitar playing!" Daddy exclaimed, which got them going with another thread. Why shouldn't Uncle E play an instrument well? He'd had the time to practice. Most people by his age are rooted down somewhere with a job and family. I'd never known Uncle E to pursue employment training, and he'd never been married.

I let out this statement under my breath: "I could wring his neck."

"What's that you say, Charmaine?" Daddy asked.

"I can't make out what you're saying, and I'm right across from you," Leo said.

"Yeah, Maine, don't mumble," Tracy John told me.

"Ne-ver mind," I enunciated.

"That was much better," Daddy said. "I heard that very clear."

What's the use?

"You don't know what it did to my heart to see him," Daddy said.

You don't know what it did to *my* heart seeing him, I thought.

It wasn't till dessert that things went from bad to, as the old folks say, worser. Daddy waxed on about Uncle E's fresh start, and I tried once again to tune out. I believe that Uncle E could change his socks, he could even change his underwear, but no amount of Daddy's words could ever convince me that Uncle E truly changed from his life of crime.

"He's really trying to get his life together, and we can't let him struggle out there all by himself. That ain't no way to treat family."

"What can we do, Daddy?" Leo asked.

"Ohhhhh!" I wailed, because it was right then that I felt a sharp pain in my side.

They all asked if I was all right, and when I said I was, Daddy drove on with his plan to aid his brother. Everything began to speed up, and I thought, Wait a minute, wait a minute. I've seen this movie before. I know exactly what's going to happen next. Whenever the subject swirled around housing and relatives, I knew what was coming.

"He can stay in my room, Unc," Tracy John volunteered.

I thought, Well, that's not as bad as it could be. A little relieved, I took a forkful of pie.

"That's kind of you, Tracy John," Daddy said, then looked at me. "But—"

The sweet potato pie went sour in my mouth.

"Uncle E will take the attic for the time being. Charmaine's room."

In that instant, Uncle Escalus had transformed my nice, fluffy romantic comedy into a three-hankie tragedy.

That night, up in the attic, I took one long last look around at my short-lived haven.

Why did Uncle E have to stay with us? There was Uncle O's place. There was Gammy's house. He had buddies, I was sure. I didn't know where, but somewhere he did. Or why couldn't he spend a few of his own bucks on housing? There was the Holiday Inn, which had lovely accommodations. He could get a room with a terrace and go out there each morning to gather his thoughts. Or he could flop in a flophouse. I hear they come complete with a hot plate.

Why was Daddy so damn generous? Always willing to give the shirt off his back (or mine).

I was going to miss my turntable, where I played to death those few albums I owned. I was going to miss my closet with the sliding door. It was almost like having my own apartment. Who would have thought that this little paradise would all disappear so quickly?

Maybe there *isn't* a God.

five

The next day before the homeroom buzzer, I filled Millicent and Cissy in on the loss of my room.

"Another cousin came to live with you?" Cissy guessed.

I closed my eyes and braced myself till I was able to bring the words to the surface. "Worse, my uncle."

"I thought he had a place," Millicent said.

I shook my head. "The other one."

"The fugitive?" Cissy asked.

My chest heaved. "Yes."

Eight-fifteen a.m. *Buzzzzzzzzz.* Those left milling about the room took their seats.

Brushing it off and turning to face forward as roll was called, Cissy said, "Well, he won't stay too long."

I shook my head. So naive. That's what the indigenous people thought when they first saw Christopher Columbus.

My heart sank even lower as I listened to the irrelevant Home and School Association pretzel-sale announcement that came over the loudspeaker: Ten cents for one, three for a quarter. Sure, that sounded like a good buy, but if you ever tried one, you'd know those pretzels were as inedible as a rubber tire. It was all the fault of the organization. They kept the pretzels in boxes all day, and by sale time, when school was dismissed, they were sweaty and the salt had risen to lumps.

Second period was English class. Our teacher, Mr. Mand, had yet to break from his monochromatic fashion statement. As if he was following some religious doctrine, he wore the same color choice in both his shirt and his tie every darn day. He passed out the slim paperback entitled *The Pearl*, written by John Steinbeck. Someone I'd heard of but never read. I flipped through this book to find that it had stressed, dog-eared pages, like it had changed hands a lot.

"Now, class, I want you to pencil your name inside the front cover. This will be yours for the next month," Mr. Mand told us.

I looked at the cover art for a moment. It featured a man, a woman, and a child in a canoe on the vast sea. The man held a pearl that was bigger than his head. I wondered what kind of oyster could produce something like that.

I erased the name *Eric Brown* and wrote in my own.

My interest was piqued but soon crested as Mr. Mand droned on about the author's biography.

John Steinbeck was born in California.

John Steinbeck lived in California.

John Steinbeck died in New York but was buried in California.

I wished Mr. Mand had skipped all that and gotten to the juice. Like, did Steinbeck marry several times, like a lot of famous people did? Was he able to support himself from his writing or was he one of those starving artists? Did critics automatically dig him or was he panned during his literary career? Did this angst lead to drink? If so, what was his beverage of choice? How about dope? Did he take it? Ever?

"Steinbeck held socialist beliefs," our English teacher finally told us.

Jackpot, I thought, and sat up in my seat a little.

"Who knows what socialism is?" he asked.

The rest of the class was dead. Since Raymond sat next to me, my eyes asked him, *You want to take this one?*

Always the gentleman, he motioned to me to go ahead.

"It's like communism," I spoke up. "It's a system where everything is supposed to be shared."

"Exactly, Charmaine," Mr. Mand said.

Raymond winked at me.

Mr. Mand went into a deeper explanation. He told us how socialists believed that people who have studied eight years to be neurosurgeons should make the same amount of money as cashiers at Pantry Pride.

"If being a doctor didn't give you a lot of money, who would want to be a doctor?" someone from the third row came alive to ask.

"People who want to help sick people," Raymond said, and was promptly laughed at.

I wanted to jump to Raymond's defense, but before I could say anything, someone else asked how much would pro athletes earn under socialism.

"The same as a cashier," the teacher said.

Demetrius McGee looked up from the comic book he'd been sneak reading. "How about Don Cornelius?"

"Who?" Mr. Mand asked.

"He's on *The Soooooooul Train*," someone from the fourth row called out.

"Oh, the same as a cashier."

"So all those big celebrities wouldn't have their mansions?"

"Not unless everyone had a mansion," Mr. Mand said.

"There's not enough money or space for everyone to have a mansion," a girl from the second row said.

Mr. Mand looked over the top of his glasses at us. "Then no one would have a mansion."

Dinah Coverdale, Demetrius's current girlfriend, gave a flick to her long, straight, amber-colored hair and said dryly, "That would never work in America."

"Our military practices it," I said, and went on to explain what my brother Horace had told me. He said that a married private with three kids had a bigger take-home paycheck than a sergeant who lived stag. And whether you had dependents or not, on most bases, everyone got their housing provided for them in identical little rose-colored houses.

"Excellent point, Charmaine," Mr. Mand said.

Dinah made a prune face at me.

Excellent, Charmaine, Raymond wrote in his notebook.

"If the United States Army can share and share alike, why can't the rest of us?" Mr. Mand asked.

Most continued to jeer, which I didn't understand. This was humble Dardon, Pennsylvania, after all. I knew for a fact that no one here lived on a luxury estate, or had even seen one up close. Still, there was this undercurrent, a type of righteous indignation. It swelled until the air was thick with it. It was unsettling, like being in a horror flick. Only, instead of zombies, I was surrounded by a swarm of crazed, greedy, foaming-at-the-mouth capitalists. Didn't they know that in a socialist system, we, the working class, would gain? I did some quick math in my head and figured we had not much (if anything) to lose.

The class batted the idea around a bit more and then Mr. Mand told us to read the first ten pages of *The Pearl* for homework.

six

The beer distributor on Church Lane had lots of cardboard boxes that it discarded on a regular basis. One day I brought a few home and took them to the attic. I borrowed Daddy's duct tape and a red Magic Marker. I began boxing up my things and printing on them: CHARMAINE'S STUFF. PLEASE DON'T TOUCH.

"That's rude," Leo said from over my shoulder.

Not having heard him come up the stairs, I was startled. "I wrote *please*."

"Uncle E's not going to bother your stuff. He's not a criminal."

"That must be why he's wanted by the police."

He qualified. "He's not a *criminal* criminal."

"Leo, he is a *criminal criminal* criminal."

He put his finger in the air as if to make a grand point. "He's not a *criminal criminal criminal* criminal."

Someone had to put a stop to this, so I said, "All right, I give."

He smirked. "I knew you'd say uncle."

Say uncle? I thought. I'm *crying* uncle.

Leo began tapping in his sneakers in the vast open space that my packing created in the room.

As I continued making labels, my brother did some spiral dance thing. I didn't know the correct terminology for it, but I knew it made me dizzy just looking at him.

"You never like to share, Maine."

He had some nerve coming up here, not helping, dancing, and telling me that.

"I never like to share?" I asked.

"That's what I just said."

That did it. I put down that duct tape and stepped to my eleven-month-younger brother. "How come I'm always the one who has to give up my room?"

He stopped twirling. Even with his chin up, he was a few inches shorter than me. "How attached could you be to this room? You were only up here for a few weeks."

I growled. "Exactly, exactly."

"You keep agreeing with me. What's the big deal? Daddy said it's just till the end of March."

"It's not even February."

"February's right around the corner and is the shortest month. Besides, it's not even like you have to share a room with me this time."

My eyes narrowed. "I'm still displaced."

Before he stormed out of the room, Leo snapped at me.

43

"Our uncle needs a place to stay, Maine. Don't be so hard-hearted."

I threw up my arms; there was no use. Just like Mr. Mand, Leo had some serious left leaning going on.

Later that afternoon, I entered my temp room and Tracy John breezed by me saying, "Make yourself to home." Despite the circumstance, I felt it was nice to be welcomed. But as I took a look around, my glad expression turned to a frown. It wasn't just the poster of Tony Dorsett on the wall. Or the Jim Brown poster on the wall. Or even the poster of Lynn Swann on the wall.

I looked in the closet. Tracy John had his helmet and shoulder pads and toys and puzzles there.

I looked in the drawers: He had all his boy's size-eight clothing there.

I looked under the bed. He had a bin that was brimming with his shoes and sneakers there.

That slickster! Tracy John hadn't moved his things to the side one inch to make room for me.

I called to him and received a bored "Yeah?" in return.

"Could you come in here for a minute?" I asked him. After a few moments, Tracy John arrived, wearing his customary bright-eyed, innocent look.

I grabbed his football, shaking it in front of him. "How am I supposed to live around all this paraphernalia?"

"What did you call this?" Tracy John asked.

"Paraphernalia!"

Tracy John took it out of my hands. "This is a football."

So there I was in my makeshift Dallas Cowboys–oriented room, just like a prisoner back inside after a short furlough. I pushed the irony of my current surroundings to the back of my mind and took out the book from English class. I always enjoyed reading at times like these because books made me feel like I was escaping. *The Pearl* opened with a picturesque view of Kino and his family. They were enjoying a porridge breakfast when this loving portrait was shattered as a scorpion crept into their adobe hut and stung Kino's baby son. Panicked, Kino rushed the infant into town to get medical care. Unfortunately, the doctor had nothing but money on his mind. Since Kino had no funds, he wouldn't examine Kino's son.

He sent his servant to the entrance to say he wasn't in.

Kino got so mad that he smashed his fist against the iron gate.

By this point I was hooked, and I probably would have read past the assigned pages to the end of the book if I hadn't gotten a phone call. It was Raymond. Since I didn't have a line of my own, I stretched the cord into the hallway, for privacy. We talked and laughed until Ma came by and told me to wrap it up.

Raymond and I did that "you hang up first, no, you hang up first" thing until Ma made her second round and a second order.

I went back to Tracy John's old room (my new room) and then it started. The music from above. Uncle E had come in while I was on the phone, and he settled into his new home, the attic, with a song. Yes, he had the un-mitigated gall to start up with his hit parade.

I would say this was the last straw, but who was I kidding? I'd been strawless since Uncle E first reappeared at our door. As one dreamy ballad melted into another heartfelt standard, I felt my head come that much closer to exploding. Since this was a live performance and not a TV show, there was no turning down the volume. Despite it all, I found myself nodding off. I thought, Well, I guess there's nothing I can do, at 10:25 p.m., against the winds of change.

Uncle E was up and I was down. He'd won this round, but I hadn't given up on having my day of victory.

seven

"I hope I don't keep you up." I overheard my deadbeat creep uncle talking to Ma the next morning. "I'm just so used to strumming a few songs before bed."

Good God, was there no avoiding him? He was right at the kitchen table. How was I supposed to enjoy my breakfast looking at his mug? I encroached upon the room with a frozen smile and a quick wave.

"It's delightful to hear your music, Escalus," Ma said, and urged me to agree. "Isn't it soothing, Charmaine?"

I opened the fridge door. "It's like a glass of warm milk."

Just then another fan club member entered the room. "Uncle E," Tracy John said, and walked right into his open arms. "Are you going to sing every night?"

"Oh, he couldn't do that, Tracy John," Ma said. "He'd wear out his voice."

"One could hope," I said under my breath. Luckily, my comment went unheard.

"You know, taking up the guitar again was the best thing I could have done," Uncle E said. "Before I did, I felt so pent up, I felt like there was a rock band in my head—"

A rock band in his head? That sounded like something diagnosable. I wondered if those voices told him to shoplift from Value City.

"My blood pressure was sky-high."

Ma nodded and said, "A lot of us have high blood pressure."

"We sure do," Tracy John agreed.

"As a matter of fact," Uncle E said, "music lowers blood pressure."

Well, if that didn't take the whole biscuit. How lucky to have three doctors in one household. I don't know how I could have missed the eight years Tracy John spent attaining MD status.

The next thing I knew, Uncle E had pulled his guitar out.

He sang that song "Cool Water," a melodrama about two men stuck in the desert who kept seeing mirages. The amusing part was the over-the-top chorus, "He's a devil, not a man, / And he spreads the burnin' sand / With water, cool, clear water."

Ma gushed, "Your music is like music to my ears."

"I couldn't say it better myself, Ma." I manufactured

enthusiasm as I faced them; then I turned my back and rolled my eyes in safety.

I slipped away with my Rice Krispies and sat in the alcove.

Leo came down the steps and heard the *snap, crackle, pop* emitted from my bowl. "What are you doing eating here on the steps?" he asked.

"That jailbird has taken over the kitchen," I said.

Leo raised his fist in the air and shouted, "That's the spirit!"

eight

"Maine used to be in Leo's room but then she got her ladytime," Tracy John said, despite my wild gesturing to him to cut it. We were in public, after all. More importantly, we were out with my boyfriend.

"Ladytime?" Raymond asked.

"That's what Auntie told me it's called," Tracy John said. As if that wasn't bad enough, he added, "It comes once a month."

When he finally clammed up, I explained, "Horace going into the service opened up a room."

"So you used to live with your brother?" Raymond asked, oblivious to my meltdown.

"Yes." Though I had too much melanin in my skin to blush, I still felt the need to duck my head down.

"Now that Uncle E is with us, I'm with Leo," Tracy John continued.

Raymond nodded along, but I would have given a million pennies for his thoughts on the matter. Did it cross his mind that the Upshaws had a hint of kookiness? Thankfully, the topic shifted as the waitress came by to drop off menus and a basket of breadsticks.

"Spider-Man," Tracy John began. "Does it get boring never eating meat?"

"There are a lot of things you can eat instead of meat."

"Like what?" Tracy John asked, settling back in the booth.

"Legumes."

Tracy John asked, "What's that?"

I told my cousin legumes meant beans, which caused him to spring into that odious jingle: "Beans, beans are good for your heart—"

I wasn't going to let this get out of control. I talked over him. "Don't finish that rhyme, Tracy John."

Baffled, Raymond asked, "How does the rest go?"

How sheltered could he be? "You really don't know what he's talking about?" I asked.

"No, but I like poetry."

Tracy John took a breadstick out of the basket. "Do you like poems about bad air?"

"All right, Tracy John," I said.

Raymond chuckled at us both and volunteered to recite his own verse. "Let me see if I can make one up just off the cuff. Roses are red—"

Tracy John leaned on his elbow. "I've heard this before."

"Violets have beards," Raymond continued, then

paused to think for a moment before coming up with the next line. "Do you think I'm weird?"

"Yes," Tracy John answered.

After ordering, Tracy John tugged at Raymond. "Can a plane land somewhere where there's dinosaurs?"

I gritted my teeth at him. "Are you going to start that again?"

An excellent mimic, Tracy John gnashed his teeth back at me. "I saw it on TV."

"Was that on last Saturday night?" Raymond asked.

Tracy John nodded.

"I know what you were watching. That was *The Twilight Zone.*"

My exclamation of "What? Tracy John, you know you're not supposed to be up that late!" collided with Raymond's "I love that one! I've seen that episode a dozen times."

I wagged my pointer finger at Tracy John. "Wait till I tell Ma you're staying up till all hours of the night over Basil's house."

He stuck out his tongue, then said, "You tell everything, Maine."

"I think the writers of that show were playing around with the idea of how time changes during travel," Raymond said. "Why, some states are even split. It's nine o'clock by one end of the state, and ten o'clock the other. Depending on where you fly, you could actually go back in time. The show exaggerated that fact and had people landing in prehistoric times."

Tracy John gave him a confused look.

"Where did you say Horace is stationed?" Raymond asked.

"Hawaii."

Raymond checked his watch and made a calculation. "That's Pacific Standard time—which would make it a quarter after five in the morning."

"How do you know?" Tracy John asked.

"Because it's 10,145 miles away, give or take," Raymond said confidently.

Tracy John looked at me. "He's good."

After that, Raymond really strode into action. He outlined how the world revolved around the sun, and then he went into others of Galileo's theories, and that's where I got lost.

My cousin, however, kept nodding and seemed to be following along. He asked Raymond, "How come there are pictures of dinosaurs?"

"They're not from a camera. They are sketches, Tracy John," Raymond told him. His voice radiated adult authority. Then he said that confusions such as Tracy John's were very common. He told us about Orson Welles, who read *The War of the Worlds* over the radio and made the people of New Jersey go into a panic, thinking aliens were actually invading Earth.

"Boy, they were really dumb," Tracy John said.

I laughed. This, coming from the kid who until just a moment ago was afraid of running into a pterodactyl.

Next, Tracy John decided to really take advantage of Raymond's fountain of knowledge. He came out with both barrels blazing.

"How come glasses of water with ice in them sweat after a while?"

"Where do stars go during the day?"

And my favorite, "If electricity is in the air, how come Unc has to pay an electric bill?"

To each question, Raymond supplied not just any old answer but an informed one. I was in awe of his encyclopedic recall and played Watson to his Holmes.

Later, at the movies, Tracy John sat between us. Though we'd just eaten, we shared a big tub of super-buttery, somewhat salty popcorn. How could you see a flick without it?

Despite being made in the thirties, *The Adventures of Robin Hood* was in color. It starred the dashing Errol Flynn as the swashbuckler of Sherwood Forest. I loosely knew the story of how Robin stole from the rich and gave to the poor, but I still hated the part when the sheriff of Nottingham dropped his weapon and our hero gave the villain a chance to pick it up, because it never worked the other way around when Robin lost the upper hand. It was still quite a welcome respite from those disaster films that were out right now, like *Earthquake*, *The Poseidon Adventure*, and *The Towering Inferno*. Whose bright idea was it that the public wanted a secondhand view of a catastrophe? Besides, vintage movie houses like this had a better ambiance: the red carpet, the chandeliers, the ushers in full uniform. Best of all, the floor wasn't sticky with spilled soda like at the Sameric downtown.

Tracy John seemed amused during the show, and at its conclusion I asked him, "Did you like Robin Hood, Tracy John?"

"I guess," he said, "but how come he had a dress on?"

Raymond and I chuckled at that, and then burst out laughing when he added, "He had on stockings too."

nine

Unfortunately, you really can't increase your chest size through exercise, just the underlying muscles. But when you're barely an A-cup, every little bit helps. As I disrobed for the night, I caught sight of how tiny I still was and realized that I'd better get to it.

I assumed the position. I concentrated. I envisioned myself at least a double-D as I squeezed my hands together. I closed my eyes, and when I reopened them, I saw Tracy John staring at me.

"What are you doing?" he asked.

I crossed my arms over my chest and scooted him back into Leo's room.

"I want my red shirt," he said.

"Why don't you take everything out of the room that you need, so you don't have to keep coming in here for everything?"

"He doesn't have to do that," Leo said. "You said yourself this is only a temporary move."

"Yeah," Tracy John told me, and walked around me back into my/his room.

Leo eyed me up and down, suppressing a laugh. "You need to eat a bucket of lard, Maine."

"Leo, you can stick your entire head in a bucket of lard."

When I finally turned in, I heard it. Uncle E's music. I had to hand it to him. For someone who had been through fire and rain, his voice was remarkably clear and smooth, like polished glass. He found that one right pitch and didn't veer up or down from that mark, and he accompanied himself beautifully on the guitar. Listening was like watching a lazy river. Too bad he'd chosen a jump song that required vocal acrobatics. He was a romantic tenor, after all, and his voice was suited for slower songs. I was no record mogul, but I did know something about music.

All throughout elementary school, I was in choir. The only reason I signed up was because Millicent and Cissy wanted me to join with them. From grades one through six, I was under the tutelage of Mrs. Mary Elizabeth Connelly, the director. She wore thick makeup, and I imagined she must have been very pretty in her youth, and this was her way of trying to hold on. She had raised knuckles due to arthritis but that did not stop her from tirelessly banging on the keys. She also was unswayed by the fact that the neighborhood had flipped ethnically. She carried on like it was still primarily Irish American.

Though we were of African descent, and thus had never dined on corned beef and cabbage, we performed numbers like "Oh Me Name Is McNamara, I'm the Leader of the Band" and "Will You Go, Lassie, Go?" (which, contrary to our initial belief, had to do with a woman, not a dog).

The look on Daddy's face was priceless during the end-of-year concert. He said something that I didn't understand the humor of at the time, but now I do. Our last song was the famous "Tooralooraloora." Daddy commented, "I've heard of Black Irish, but that was ridiculous."

Now that I get his joke, I wondered: If I dragged my bony ass to Ireland, would I be considered a bonny lass?

At any rate, that was the stuff Uncle E should have stuck to. I was convinced that he could tear up "Danny Boy."

The fine drizzle that had been going on all day finally threatened to turn into a storm by the end of school. Of course, Raymond thought ahead as he waited for me by the monument in front of the school. He had brought his big, green mushroom umbrella. He rushed toward me as I began to walk in his direction.

"Maine," Millicent and Cissy called. They were under Millicent's pink flat-topped covering.

I looked in their direction.

"Hey, I was just going over Raymond's. Why don't you come too?"

"No thanks. We don't want to be a third wheel," Millicent said.

Raindrops spat on my face, and I ducked my head under Raymond's covering. "You won't be a third wheel," I said.

As they came closer, I moved out from Raymond's umbrella and got soaked while standing in the middle.

"No, we'd be fourth wheels," Cissy said.

"Cars have four wheels," Raymond said.

Millicent and Cissy still shook their heads.

I guess King Solomon would have suggested splitting me in half, but without his wisdom, I made up my own mind. Since I already had plans with Raymond, I decided to go with him. A similar thing had happened the other day when we saw *Robin Hood*. Millicent and Cissy were invited but they said they didn't want to be hangers-on. Even after I assured them that Tracy John was coming along, they declined.

Not until quite some time later did it dawn on me that I'd spent less and less time with Millicent and Cissy. How do people who have gobs of close friends work this out? How do they keep everything straight? Moreover, how are you supposed to hang out with people if they always say no?

"Some other time," Millicent said.

"Tomorrow?" I asked.

They just smiled. They took the shortcut through the William B. Evans Elementary School playground. By then, the rain was really coming down.

In life there are provincial, local yokels and then there are wild-minded adventurers. Even though I rarely went five miles outside Dardon, Pennsylvania, I was convinced that I was the latter. But each visit to the Newell household made me rethink that.

Maybe if they weren't so vegetarian. I went the entire evening feeling forsaken, thrown into all this "health." In my family, even the collard greens were seasoned with fatback, so the Newell way of eating really threw me. Besides that, where were the rolls like Ma made for every meal? Where was the rice or, at the very least, potatoes?

Of course, you don't go over someone's house to eat. It isn't about cuisine; it's about inspection. Them of me. Me of them.

Mr. and Mrs. Newell both wore glasses and had impeccable manners. It was so bizarre to spend supper with no one reaching across the table and everyone speaking in complete, well-modulated sentences.

Mr. Newell wore a necktie and long sleeves, on this, a Tuesday.

I bet he didn't have a tattoo on his arm like my daddy did.

Judging by her ruled forehead and crinkly eyes, I had no doubt Mrs. Newell was of age when she married, unlike my ma.

They both started nearly each sentence to me with "So Raymond tells us…" After that ran its course, our constricted talk was limited to the tight perimeters of "How's school?"

After forcing down the roots and sprouts that they called dinner, I volunteered to help with the dishes but was glad when Mrs. Newell said I didn't have to.

We moved into the living room, where Mr. Newell said, "Raymond tells us your uncle is a musician."

I shot a distressed look to Raymond, who appeared just as surprised by the comment as I was.

"Yes, he plays the guitar and sings, but right now he works at a furniture store," I said.

"He must be at a crossroads. What line of work is he looking to get into?" Mr. Newell asked.

Daddy told us, "Always tell the truth but don't strip down to your long johns." I gulped and blurted out, "I don't know. As long as I've known him, he always picked up a few things here and there."

Home at last, I was safe with a hunk of dead flesh on my plate.

I didn't bother to heat it up; I would have eaten that chicken piece with ice cubes on it. When Leo caught me gnawing on a drumstick, he asked, "Didn't you just come back from dinner at Raymond's?"

I held up one finger asking for a moment. I swallowed and then said, "Yes."

Like *this* was weird behavior.

ten

Our mailman always delivered by a quarter to three. On days that I came straight home, I'd see a small pile of letters on the table. I customarily regarded this with low interest. Aside from an occasional card from Horace, most everything was for Daddy, or for just plain "Resident."

As I cleared things away for supper, I noticed one was addressed to me. It was from the Thomas Sharpe Talent Agency.

"Ma, how come you didn't tell me?" I called to her in the kitchen.

"What?" she called back.

I frowned. "Never mind."

I held the thick envelope to my chest, thinking this was it.

I ripped the letter open. Sure enough, the first line

read "Congratulations." Was there ever a more beautiful word in the English language? I let out a yowl.

"Stop your yelling in the house, Charmaine," Ma told me.

I ran into the other room. "A modeling agency wants to see me."

Leo cocked his head to the side, refusing to be taken in. "Yeah, right."

"Look for yourself." I handed him the letter.

Leo perused the note without much expression.

"This just says that you are chosen as a semifinalist. A regional semifinalist."

I growled and walked toward Ma to show her.

"What do you think?"

She read over the letter I held out to her. "Oh, that's nice, Charmaine."

"Nice? Nice?" I asked her.

When she didn't give me anything more, I sped out of the room.

I knew one person I could count on to give the reaction that I wanted. I sought Raymond's number.

"I want to thank you, thank you, thank you, thank you, Raymond. I want to thank you so much. I owe this all to you."

He said something I'd never forget: "It's your face, Maine."

There was something about the way he said it was my face that went to my head.

I guessed I was beautiful. Or not. What difference did it make? I was a winner.

I rang Cissy, and her sister told me that she was over Millicent's. I dialed Millicent's number and was informed by her grandma that Millicent and Cissy had just gone to the five-and-dime store. I had to relay the message or else I'd rupture, so I went ahead and did.

"Who's gonna be a model?" Millicent's grandma asked.

"*Me!*" I spoke up because she was hard of hearing.

"You?" she asked, baffled. "I thought I was talking to Charmaine."

"*You are!*"

"What's that you say?"

"This *is* Charmaine."

"Of course, honey."

At that point, I gave up.

"Congratulations on your reward," Tracy John said during supper.

"Thank you, Tracy John, but it's not a reward," I corrected him, and explained the difference between a reward and an award.

"What do they mean by 'tristate'?" Leo asked. "Does that include New York?"

"Don't make no difference which three states it is," Daddy answered for me.

Leo wasn't budging. "New York has a lot of people in it."

"Now, now, let's not nitpick, Leo. Charmaine, this is wonderful news."

"Thank you, Daddy," I said, because right then he

made me believe he was on my side. Later that night, during my eavesdropping, I would learn something different.

"Modeling? Well, if that don't beat all. How did she get mixed up in such a thing?"

"Peyton, that nice boy she's been seeing sent in her name."

"Miss Sweet Thang, that is the last thing I'd ever, ever expect her to be interested in. I thought she would do something to help people."

From behind the door, I wanted to scream, *Models help people. They help millions of people pick out clothes, and choose what makeup they want to wear. Models couldn't be any more helpful to humanity!*

Daddy bemoaned some more. "I had hoped Charmaine would do something worthwhile with her life."

Modeling was as substantial as what Leo and Tracy John were into. I'd never heard of a tap dancer becoming a Nobel Laureate or a football player finding a cure for cancer.

I listened on as Daddy ran my dreams down to the dogs, wondering how could he be against modeling, such a nice, wholesome American institution.

When the subject changed, I retired to my room, thinking how shortsighted Daddy was. This could be big! We could all be rich! Not just kind-of-sort-of rich, I was talking so much money the Rockefellers would be hitting us up for a loan! All for my occasional thirty-second commercial and my periodic stroll down the runway.

eleven

The Bible says it is easier for a camel to fit through the eye of a needle than for a rich person to make it into Heaven.

But what about models? Wouldn't they be the exception?

They make a lot of money, and they are thin enough to fit through a needle's eye.

"There's a star!" Millicent and Cissy sang out as I entered homeroom.

I put both hands up as if to quell the public outburst. Giggles and hugs followed. I guess Millicent's grandma had been able to understand some of what I was saying.

After loved ones and friends heard my good news, who was left but acquaintances? Next period, our regular math teacher, Mrs. Trice, was absent, so I had the opportunity to tell some of my classmates.

Unfortunately, Dinah was in earshot. She had the nerve to stick out her already prominent chest and proclaim: "The people at that agency must be between eye exams."

I thought before I responded to her. Did I really want to get this rivalry kicked up again? After all, Dinah and I had been existing on each other's periphery since Christmas break, pretending that we had no history. Though she occasionally made faces, Dinah had till now taken a hiatus from making rude comments to me.

Against my better judgment, I pushed my chest out too (though the visual effect wasn't nearly as convincing) and fired back, "Maybe you're just jealous."

"Of what?" she asked. Then she went into her other trademark, she swished her hair.

A voice came from far behind me. "I think Charmaine has all the makings of a model."

Every neck craned in the voice's direction. I turned to look, but I didn't know how I couldn't have recognized that voice as Demetrius's. Why was he, of all people, supporting me? Who would have thought that my fake boyfriend of last year, who dogged me out, would ever be of use?

My eyes went back to Dinah. After another swish of her mane, she asked, "Who would want a magazine with *you* on the cover?"

Before I had a chance to mount a defense, that same voice from the back of the room said, "One thing's for sure, Dinah, *you* weren't picked."

The class clamored with laughs and claps.

Dinah got all huffy and tomato-soup red.

Right then, the substitute came back in the room, and we went back to pretending we were deciphering word problems.

After class, Demetrius caught up with me. "Hey, Maine, I did a good job sticking up for you just now."

"I didn't need your help. I can take care of myself."

"Maybe we got off on the wrong foot," he said.

That made me half turn my head to him. "You mean with me doing all your homework last term, and you treating me like crap."

"Yep, that wrong foot. Think of this as a new day."

"Every day's a new day, Demetrius."

"I mean between us." He smiled, showing his shiny teeth against his dark complexion. "My half brother and your cousin are like best friends. It doesn't make sense that we barely speak to each other."

"It doesn't?" I asked, failing to follow his logic.

He placed his hand on my shoulder. "Besides, going out with the same person is so dull. Don't you think?"

I brusquely shook his hand off. "Maybe it's who you choose to go out with."

Off by the lockers, Dinah cleared her throat and stomped her foot. She might as well have stood on her head for all the attention Demetrius gave her. Her gaze went to me and went icy.

What to do? The good side of me told me, *Don't be petty*.

The bad side said, *Make her suffer*.

Just then, the bell for the next class rang, and we went our separate ways.

The next day, after chemistry, Demetrius tried to talk me up again. This time he told me about the talent classes he'd taken when he lived in Baltimore. He said he had studied not only modeling but acting. When he said that, something clicked. Acting? I never knew he was interested in that, but the more I thought of it, the more I realized it would be perfect for him, with his vast background in plagiarism. It only made sense that he'd be good at saying words that someone else wrote in a way that someone else directed him to.

Demetrius's smile was wide and frank. A few steps behind him, Dinah's spooky gray eyes burned with indignation.

Many of my classmates would rush home after school to watch *General Hospital* or *Guiding Light*. No need that day, we were smack-dab in the middle of the corridor. Dardon Junior High had its own home-grown soap opera moment. And in this episode, I was the lead.

twelve

Tracy John wheeled his bike—which used to be Horace's before it was briefly mine and before it was Leo's—into the back shed.

I noticed the care he took as he placed an old blanket on it.

"Don't worry about that old thing, I'll buy you a new one."

"You'll get me a new bike?" he asked.

"I'll get you *two* new bikes."

His penny-colored eyes widened. "How about five bikes?"

"Deal," I said.

A mischievous smile grew on his face. "How about ten bikes?"

I pinched him on the cheek. "You got it."

"How about twenty bikes?"

I wagged my finger back and forth at him in playful admonishment. "Don't get greedy."

We had a good laugh together as we walked inside the house. Leo interrupted our mirth. "Have you two lost your minds?"

"I can assure you that we are both quite sane and soon we all will be quite rich."

"How?" Leo asked.

Tracy John broke ranks and asked me, "Yeah, how?"

I breathed on my fingernails and buffed them on my blouse. "You know I won that modeling contest."

Leo said, "You can donate my cut to charity."

That very same day, a Saturday, Ma and Tracy John accompanied me to a consultation at the agency. The place was located on Chestnut Street near the Broad Street intersection in one of those big, stately buildings with a doorman and everything. We took the stomach-flipping elevator ride to the twenty-first floor and ambled into the kind of place where you didn't want to touch anything for fear that you might leave a smudge.

A woman with arched brows and a dark green skirt suit stepped from behind the desk and asked Ma, "May I get you a cup of coffee?"

Tracy John raised his hand. "I'll have a cup."

"No, thank you," Ma said.

The woman in green next led us over the glistening marble floor to a large room that was already filling up with young ladies and their guardians. This was the

71

competition, other tristate hopefuls who had received the summons. I eyed them closely and took account of their movements. The way their bones pushed against their skin. (Nobody wants a bone but a dog, old folks always say.) I also studied the manner in which they tossed their small heads or sucked their lower lips. One loomed against the wall. Another's foot was tapping the floor. Another was pondering her nails, bending her hands and bringing each one close to her eyes, looking for a fault.

The woman from the front office counted our heads. I got a better look at her this time and noted how her hair was drawn away tightly from her face and was held by two strong combs. With her eye hollows and soaring bone structure, I wondered if she was a former model. "Ann Marie Sharpe-Adams will be right with us," she announced.

At last the presentation started. A screen came down in front of the room just as a vision swept in from the hall. A heavily bejeweled woman entered, draped in white chiffon. "Good afternoon, stars of tomorrow," she said.

Everyone clapped.

She went on to say that she was the granddaughter of Thomas Sharpe and that the agency had been around since 1926. She directed our eyes to the screen, the lights went out, and an aquamarine-eyed woman appeared in a blouse so sheer it was see-through.

Ma scrambled over me to cover Tracy John's eyes.

"You can see her—" was all Tracy John was able to get out before his mouth too, was covered.

Next a wispy brunette, followed by a cherubic-faced blonde, materialized on screen. Then another blonde, this time an icy Kim Novak type, then another blonde, then a freckled redhead, then a fiery auburn-haired lass.

I kept waiting for the sisters. We were definitely represented in the room, about one out of every five, just over the blacks-to-whites ratio of the U.S. population. By this time, Thomas Sharpe's granddaughter had shown thirty slides, yet no one of my background had been showcased.

Finally, a picture came on of a young lady with raven eyes and hair and deeply pigmented skin. It wasn't Naomi Sims or Beverly Johnson. She was a model I'd never seen before, but that was all right. I nodded and clapped loudly.

Picking up on this, Ms. Sharpe-Adams said, "The ethnic market is hot right now. We are definitely looking for more ethnic faces."

Tracy John tugged at Ma. "Auntie, are we ethnic?"

Next came a picture of a woman in an itsy-bitsy teeny-weeny string bikini. Though Ma didn't shield Tracy John from that photo, it gave me another thing to worry about. If I ever did make it in modeling, I'd have to put in a modesty clause regulating how much skin I would show. I don't want to be photographed in see-through clothing or skimpy swimwear. The last thing I wanted to be known as was a bombshell. I wouldn't want a bunch of strange men drooling over me. I am a lady.

The next couple of shots featured models standing in front of a mountain. There were some ohhhhhhs and a couple of ahhhhhs.

"We strongly suggest you use our photographer for your portfolio."

She flipped the pictures very quickly now. "Aren't these lovely?"

"How much are you charging for this portfolio?" someone's mom asked.

"A mere three hundred ninety-five dollars plus forty dollars for the makeup session."

The air got heavy.

Ma leaned back and placed her hand over her heart. The woman who'd asked the question grabbed her daughter's hand, and together they left the room.

"Do we get to keep the negatives?" someone else asked.

"That will be an extra twenty per slide."

Two more mothers left with their daughters in tow.

"What else is highly recommended?" someone asked.

"Before we send you out on auditions, you have to take our classes, which run ten-fifty per session, or ten weeks for a hundred dollars. That's a savings of five dollars!" she said as if generosity dripped from her pores.

The crowd thinned more.

My heart sank. Why was it that everything cost money?

Life is an open sea and then it's not. There have been big stars who have leapfrogged over all these primary steps. In Raymond's Hollywood book, it told of the famed actress Lana Turner, who was discovered sipping a malted at Schwab's drugstore. Talk about luck. If you lived in

L.A., you were more likely to run into those people, but what were the odds of me meeting a movie producer on the number thirteen trolley?

More insurrections followed as people asked pointed questions about money, money, money.

Mrs. Sharpe-Adams spoke over them. "These were taken by our photographer, the fabulous Pierre Brochère."

I got a sinking feeling.

I felt like the lovely honeybee that passes the fragrant garden of daffodils and lands in a pile of crap.

"Why can't we take our own pictures?" someone asked.

"I'm sure they won't come out like *this*," Mrs. Sharpe-Adams responded. Next came something else that the letter had promised: our one-on-one consultations. I saw plaques on the wall of the many accolades Thomas Sharpe had won. There were also pictures of celebs like Farrah Fawcett and Robert Redford.

Sharpe's chiffoned granddaughter had brows that climbed to tapered peaks above her brown eyes. At the sight of me she exclaimed, "Where did you get those cheekbones?"

After shaking her hand with a firm grip, I sat down between my mother and my cousin.

"I can't believe you have been waiting this long. You could have been modeling for years," she told me.

"She's only a teenager," Tracy John said.

I pressed my knee heavily against his, as if to tell him *Cut it*.

"She could have taken up modeling when she was your age or even younger. We have clients as young as six months."

"That's a baby." Tracy John folded his arms across his chest. "Babies can't walk or talk. How are they gonna model?"

"They can still be in front of the cameras. What are *you* waiting for?"

"Me?" Tracy John uttered the first humble word in his life.

She handed a brochure to Ma.

"I've been thinking of starting a class just for little boys. However, we probably won't get it going until the fall."

"In the fall, Tracy John likes to play peewee football. That's enough of his time occupied," Ma told her.

"Are you sure?" Ms. Sharpe-Adams asked. "This is important."

"So is football," Tracy John said.

Her smile didn't fade; in fact, it grew. "That's a pity; you definitely show great potential," she said to my cousin.

I nodded, agreeing wholeheartedly. My little cousin reeked of star quality.

She directed the questions that followed to Ma. "Do you have any other family members, Mrs. Upshaw?"

Ma told her Leo had dance lessons.

"How about Horace?" Tracy John asked.

Ma patted Tracy John on his head. "Horace can't do this, honey. He's in the military."

"Where is he stationed?" Ms. Sharpe-Adams asked. "We have offices all around the world."

I sighed. There I was, lost in the shuffle at my own interview. After her comment about my cheekbones, Sharpe's granddaughter seemed to all but forget I was in the room.

She went on to explain the different payment plans, which knocked off five percent of the enrollment price per family member that joined.

"It's never too late, Mrs. Upshaw. We also have adult classes." She winked at us.

During the trolley ride home, Tracy John unfolded the accordion-like brochure and read it closely.

I shook my head at him and Ma caught me. "At least he's going over the material. That's what you should be doing. You know what they say, Charmaine. Fools rush in."

Tracy John looked up from the paperwork and agreed, "Yeah, Maine, fools."

I turned to the window. The trolley went underground.

The inside lights came on, but I had to wait five more stops for there to be a light at the end of the tunnel.

thirteen

During supper, I told Daddy, "The head of the agency said I have good cheekbones."

"What do bad cheekbones look like?" Leo asked.

Daddy shook his head. "Enough, Leo. Your sister has a nice face."

Here we went again with that word.

"Charmaine also has a nice speaking voice," Ma said as she passed around the peas and carrots.

Nice. Nice. Nice. My parents were trying to make my head explode.

Leo reached for a roll. "How could they tell her voice by looking at her picture?"

I gave Leo a dirty look. I'd always heard that it was lonely at the top, but I thought you'd have to get to the top first to be lonely. "You know, a lot of models move into acting."

"Is that right?" Daddy sliced into the baked flounder. "Well, sounds like you had quite an experience."

"It may not be over yet," I said.

"The classes cost ten dollars and fifty cents," Ma said.

Daddy whistled. "That's out of sight."

Leo shook his head. "If that's what you get from winning a competition, you better hope you don't lose one anytime soon."

"Ten dollars a class," Daddy repeated.

"And fifty cents," Tracy John said.

Leo asked, "What's the fifty cents for?"

I glowered. I knew money would stand in my way. If all of a sudden the cost of Leo's tap lessons shot up like a rocket, Daddy would find a way to cover it. If Tracy John's peewee football stuff cost a million dollars, he'd move Heaven and earth to pay for it.

I shifted my collard greens around my plate and meekly said, "Lessons could lead to millions."

"Can they guarantee that?" Leo asked.

I began to cry inside. Everyone shot me down. *Nobody loves me. No one at all.*

"Well," Daddy began, "if that's what you really want, we'll try to come up with the money for a few classes."

Ma gasped. "Peyton."

"I said a few, Miss Sweet Thang."

My heart had wings again.

"How many is that, Unc?" Tracy John asked.

"A few"—he paused and drank a swallow of water—"is a few. But Charmaine has to really investigate this place."

"Unc, that lady wanted me and Auntie to take classes," Tracy John said, and pointed to Leo. "And you and Horace."

Daddy nodded knowingly. "So they want to recruit my whole family, eh? Now, Charmaine, put on your thinking cap, what does that tell you?"

I put on a big smile and batted my eyelashes. "That we're all photogenic?"

"Come on, Maine," Leo said. "They've never even seen me or Horace."

"Leo, didn't I say that was enough from you?" Daddy said.

"This thing stinks to high Heaven, Daddy," Leo said in a voice rich with righteous indignation.

I turned to Tracy John. He held his nose and said, "Pew."

I flipped back to Daddy, who said, "Charmaine is no dummy. I'm sure she would not let someone who tells her that she has good cheekbones pull the wool over her eyes. I trust that she wouldn't let us fall prey to a scam."

"You won't be sorry, Daddy. We'll be in Hollywood before you know it."

Daddy frowned; it wasn't often that I saw Daddy frown. "You still don't understand, Charmaine. Even if this agency wasn't suspect, Hollywood is the last place I'd want us to be."

Leo was a frowner and an eye-roller and every other gesture of disapproval known to mankind. "Hollywood? You've never even been in a school play, Maine," Leo said.

80

"That's not a prerequisite," I told him.

"Since when have you ever been interested in acting?" Leo asked.

I sighed. Did I have to explain everything? "I'm not talking about acting; I'm talking about being in the movies."

I cleared the dinner plates without a clang and met up with Ma by the sink.

"I don't know why you are suddenly so preoccupied with money. You know there's more to life than that," Ma said as she spooned out a dollop of vanilla ice cream for each helping of peach cobbler. Immediately, she followed that cliché with a story I'd heard a thousand times. She told me about how she and all of her four sisters had to share one coat. They had to take turns wearing it.

How cold does it get in Alabama, Ma? I wanted to ask, but I didn't want to ruin the flow of her favorite story. I politely listened, wondering, Why, oh why, do older people like to do this? They always made out like they walked, no, crawled, no, swam ten, no, twenty, no, a hundred miles to school. They made out like their generation had it so hard and my generation had it so easy. Ha. I had it easy? Look how tentatively Daddy agreed to fund my modeling lessons.

I placed an à la mode helping in front of Daddy and another one before Tracy John.

"You know, Cicely Tyson was nominated for an Academy Award."

"Oh, that *Sounder* was a lovely movie," Ma said.

"I liked the dog in *Sounder*," Tracy John said.

"They should have given that dog an award," Daddy said.

Tracy John laughed so hard at that, he spat out some of his ice cream.

Ma went to clean him up.

"I want to win an Emmy and a Tony and an Oscar and a Grammy and a Golden—"

"Maybe you ought to slow down with all this show business talk, Charmaine," Daddy advised over his cobbler. "See how things go after you learn more about this, because one thing is for sure: You can't go taking the cart before the horse."

Ma continued to gang up on me. "I done told her fools rush in."

"Yeah, Maine, fools," Tracy John said.

"What is the harm in—" I began.

"Maine, that's what Daddy's telling you," Leo said.

"Can I finish my sentence?" I asked heatedly.

"Charmaine, there's no need to raise your voice," Ma said.

Daddy nodded knowingly. "Charmaine, this is what I was talking about. This is exactly how it starts."

Just ten minutes ago, there'd been a glimmer of support from him. "How what starts?" I asked.

"Trust me, you don't want to get mixed up with that world," Daddy said.

"Yeah, Maine, you need to stay in *this* world," Tracy John said.

Though I felt my heart go to clear liquid, I made one last effort. "I just don't see the harm in pursuing a career in entertainment."

Daddy pointed at me with his fork. "I hope you heed my advice. Stay away from those people. They are the unhappiest people God ever created."

"They sure look happy."

"That's why they're called actors," Leo said.

I didn't care what my family thought; I knew the truth. Nobody wants a humble life; everyone craves to be pushed to the front in one way or another. I understood that not everyone can make it into the limelight, but some people do. Every single day, new famous people were in the newspaper.

Why couldn't I have what they had? It was a simple question.

I'd seen Daddy struggling, getting up before the birds every morning, and Auntie Karyn studying and studying with her big, thick medical books. That's the long way. My plan was the fast track.

The dynasty begins with me and it will be big, I thought. I will not just conquer showbiz, but one day I will franchise. First, I'd have my own jeans. I'd have my name on everyone's butt, like Levi Strauss. Then I'd move on to a line of perfume. Then snack food. What customer could resist Charmaine's Potato Chips?

My family was just the opposite of the way the saying goes. Nobody wanted to get into the act. They were too cautious and conservative. They couldn't fathom the gold mine we were sitting on.

I'd love to see Daddy in a movie. He could take the roles Billy Dee Williams was too busy for.

And Ma, well, there'd be parts for her. Ma could play someone's ma. She'd be very believable at that.

Now, what part could Tracy John play? After one glimpse, a casting director would stick my cousin's angelic, innocent face and princely bearing in a Little Lord Fauntleroy part. Wrong. That would waste his flinty personality. If I were in charge of production, I'd get a cowlick going with Tracy John's 'fro and voila, I'd give him a role where he could be a black version of Dennis the Menace.

Horace would prove versatile, but that would have to wait till his enlistment contract was complete.

And Leo, with his dancing ability, he would have been a shoo-in twenty years ago. Who made musicals anymore? Uncle E and his guitar would have the same problem.

fourteen

The next day I rethought my whole casting and ran through a totally new scenario. "Think of it, Daddy, I could emcee. Leo could showcase his dance ability. Horace could tell jokes. . . . I haven't figured out yet what Tracy John could do."

"You haven't?"

"No, not yet. But I figured we'll give him a few years before he joins the routine. Well, what do you think?"

"Charmaine, we ain't the gosh-darn Jackson Five."

It's funny he mentioned that. Millicent and Cissy were deep in mourning ever since they heard that the five brothers from Gary, Indiana, had parted company. I took the news less to heart. I was a Jackson Five fan, not a JACKSON FIVE FAN. I hated the way they made that little guy, Michael, do all the work in the group. Whose brilliant idea was that? An eleven-year-old front man who was asked to be James Brown, Jackie Wilson, and Sam Cooke all rolled into one. Talk about pressure.

Still, there was a vacancy. A space where the right act could fit in. After all, nature abhors a vacuum.

"Maine, your father already said he'd pay for some of your classes," Ma told me. "Now, let's not run this thing into the ground. I want you to find something else to talk about."

Find something else? Like that was easy. Hadn't she heard? There's no business like show business.

During English class, I observed Demetrius with skepticism as he approached, then interrupted my conversation with Raymond.

"What time should I drop by?" Demetrius asked.

Raymond's face froze in wild alarm.

"Huh?" I asked.

"To practice the commercial audition. I want to help you rehearse."

Raymond turned to me. "When did you arrange this?"

Demetrius all but stepped on Raymond's words. "How about right after school?"

"I don't even know what you're talking about," I said.

"You remember. I'll be over at three." I noticed he wasn't asking. My eyes followed him as he went to his desk; then they returned to Raymond. I swear I saw steam coming out of his ears.

Mr. Mand began his lecture. More about *The Pearl*.

Raymond wrote this in his notebook and flashed it at me: *Are you interested in him or are you interested in me?*

Did he really expect any perfidy on my part? I had barely gone out with one guy in my entire life on this earth, how could I be accused of dating two?

I tore off a small piece from the sheet I was to take notes on and scripted the words: *What do you think?*

Raymond made a face.

Mr. Mand was in the middle of making a point about the colonial structure of Mexico when he noticed something was going on between us. It couldn't have been more obvious. Raymond and I occupied seats in the front row. Mr. Mand paused for a moment and gave me a sharp look.

Oblivious, Raymond turned the paper over and wrote something on the back, then passed it to me.

I slipped it into my book as a marker. Throughout the rest of the session, I kept my eyes front. At the bell, I pulled the note out and read: *Would it pain you, Maine, to say it?*

"Say what?" I asked Raymond.

"That you are not interested in Demetrius."

"This is way past absurd. You know Mr. Mand caught us passing notes."

"All I want is an answer."

I bridled at this. "You've turned into Dr. Jekyll."

"You mean Mr. Hyde."

"Which one is the crazy one?" I asked.

"Mr. Hyde."

"Oh, then you're right."

"Is he going to come over your house?"

His question had such histrionics, such urgency, I didn't know what to say. Luckily, there was a *buzzzzzzzz*. I went to phys ed, and he went to U.S. history.

I could hardly wait for lunch, so I could relay to my two best friends what had happened. Dardon Junior High's cafeteria was serving South Philly hoagies, which Cissy and Millicent took forever waiting in line for. One look at those oily kaiser rolls made me glad that I always brought my lunch. I sat at our table alone until they came with their trays. I told them everything in a rush.

"Who's Mr. Hyde?" Cissy asked.

"Forget him. Who's right, me or Raymond?" I asked.

"Raymond," they both said.

"Huh?"

"You're only going to make things confused," Millicent said.

"How? I'm not interested in Demetrius."

"You used to be," Cissy pointed out, and took one of my Fig Newtons.

I pushed the entire package closer to her. "*Used to* means not anymore, right?"

"Think of how Raymond feels," Millicent said.

"Raymond completely overreacted," I said.

"And you wouldn't do the same?" Cissy asked. "If he was flirting with some girl?"

"I don't flirt."

"Why are you getting mixed up with Demetrius all over again? Haven't you learned your lesson?"

"All he's doing is going over some commercial ads. You know he studied acting."

Millicent took a large bite of her apple. "That must be why he's so fake."

I was doubtful Demetrius would show, so on my own I rehearsed before a mirror. I did Lauren Bacall from Raymond's book. She was only nineteen (four years and two months older than me) when she starred opposite that much older, somewhat shorter Humphrey Bogart in *To Have and Have Not*. She was a former model who never really studied acting, yet she scorched the screen with her poise and maturity. I practiced her immortal lines: "You know how to whistle, don't you? Just put your lips together and blow."

I said it a half-dozen times, emphasizing different words. I took my voice down an octave to sound worldly like Bacall. Afterwards, my throat was sore, but at least I proved to myself that I could nail it.

After that, I practiced putting on makeup. I had deep-set eyes and wore spectacles, so I really had to go some to make them pop. According to the *Glamour* magazine that I borrowed from the library, I had to outline thickly around my lids.

"What are you putting in your eye?" Tracy John asked, horrified, as he entered the room.

"I'm not putting anything in my eye," I said, and put my glasses back on. I turned away from the mirror. "How do I look?"

Tracy John came toward me, studied me closely, and concluded, "The same."

I put some blush on his cheeks.

"You look beautiful!" I said.

He tried to rub it off, but any makeup artist would have told him that just makes it worse. I asked him to stand still and blotted the blush off him with a damp cloth.

"Is it gone?" he asked.

With his bright eyes and ruddy lips, Tracy John naturally had the kind of face that cosmetics sought to create by illusion. I pushed his button nose. "It's all gone, but you are still beautiful. What's up?"

"He's back."

"Who?" I asked.

"The jive turkey," he said.

Demetrius had made a special guest appearance after all. "That's Mr. Jive Turkey to you," I said.

He led me to the stairway so we could spy on who was downstairs.

"He's not Spider-Man," Tracy John told me.

I replied, "And you're not the Green Hornet."

"What's he doing here?"

"He said he wanted to help me practice for an audition."

"What's an audition?" Tracy John asked.

After I told him, he said, "I'd like to see you in an audition."

"Follow me, then."

We came down the steps. At the sight of Tracy John, Demetrius rolled his eyes grandly. "Does he have to sit in?"

"Tracy John is more than welcome to."

Tracy John settled on the couch for all of two seconds; then he got up and ran out of the room.

"Where are you going?" I called after him. When my question went unanswered, Demetrius seemed relieved.

Tracy John came back into the room with Leo.

That really miffed Demetrius. "Don't you two have something else to do?"

"Nope," they said in unison, settling in.

Tracy John clapped his hands. "Take it from the top."

Demetrius took to the center of the room and leafed through his papers. "Here's an interesting one," he said, then lapsed into a breathing exercise and a few shoulder rolls. Finally, he read from the sheet, "I would love to stop smoking."

"When did you start?" Leo asked.

"Ohhhhhhhhh, I'm going to tell," Tracy John said.

Demetrius turned to me. "Must I put up with these interruptions?"

"Why don't you read something else, Demetrius?" I asked him.

"I guess I'll have to." He shuffled through the sheets

and pulled out a new ad. He exaggerated his inhales and exhales, did more shoulder rolls, and asked, "Are you looking for a soft drink that's crisp and clean?"

"No," Tracy John called out.

Demetrius pointed at Tracy John. "I thought you were going to keep quiet."

"You asked the question," Leo said.

Demetrius shook it off and asked, "Where was I before I was so rudely interrupted?"

What drama! "Are you looking for—" I filled in.

"I've got it," he snapped at me. More loud breathing, more shrugs.

"Why does he keep doing that?" Tracy John asked me.

"I am centering myself!" Demetrius yelled; then he took one more cleansing breath. "Now, where was I?"

When silence followed, I cast him an inquiring glance. Had he truly lost his place? Did he require a prompt?

"Are you looking for—" I began.

Finally, he went into his rendition. "Are you looking for a soft drink that's crisp and clean? Made with ten percent real fruit juice, all-new Raspberry Cola is the drink for you."

In the English language, there are thousands of subtleties. Demetrius recognized none of them. To top that off, he had stilted herky-jerky arm movements as he pantomimed the opening of the bottle and said, "Pure refreshment."

At least my brother and cousin waited till Demetrius's conclusion before erupting with laughter.

"And what is so funny?" Demetrius asked them.

Leo got ahold of himself and said, "You're not exactly convincing."

"Did I ask for a critique?"

"It's not like they booed you, Demetrius," I said.

"What do they know about talent?"

"Like we've never seen a commercial before," Leo said.

"Well, maybe that wasn't my best reading, but how can I possibly deliver a credible performance with you two constantly chiming in?"

"You ought to be used to audiences," Leo said.

"Yeah," Tracy John said.

"I've been studying since before you were born," Demetrius told Tracy John. He made a large theatrical gesture with his hand, and he bored into Leo with his eyes and said, "And I've been to New York City."

"What does that mean?" Tracy John asked.

Instead of answering his question, Demetrius kept right on with his tirade. "There is no way I can showcase my skills"—he paused and gave my brother and cousin a disparaging look—"under these conditions."

"Is that what you came here for, Demetrius, to perform? I thought you were going to coach me through an audition," I said.

He gathered up his paperwork. "It's best to follow by example, Maine. But I'm afraid I will have to deprive you of that."

"I wish you'd deprived us of the whole thing," Leo said.

Demetrius made a hasty exit stage left.

"What a spoiled brat!" Tracy John exclaimed.

I nodded. Anyone would conclude that Demetrius prancing about like he was Sidney Poitier fresh from *Guess Who's Coming to Dinner* was sure strange.

"Someone ought to give him an award," Leo said.

Tracy John and I craned our necks in his direction.

Leo said, gesturing as if to place the words in the air, "World's Worst Actor."

fifteen

Shakespeare wrote, "All the world's a stage / And all the men and women merely players." Certain that that would be the end of Demetrius's appearance in the movie of my life, I took my turn to roll my shoulders and inhale deeply, then exhale—in a sigh of relief.

However, the next day when I passed Demetrius and Dinah in the hall, he had the gall to wink at me. I drew back in horror; then I narrowed my eyes at him as if to tell him I was onto his game. Raymond was right beside me, and his tiny cramped shoulders looked agitated. He seemed more bothered than Dinah did.

Back home that afternoon, things really exploded. It started innocently enough. Tracy John told Raymond and me about the fishing trip he was going to go on with Uncle E. Out of the blue, he asked my boyfriend, "Would you like to go fishing with us?"

Raymond nodded eagerly. "Sure, that sounds like fun."

I had to laugh, and told my cousin, "Tracy John, he's just saying that to be polite."

My cousin turned to Raymond. "Are you just saying that to be polite, or do you really want to go fishing?"

"I would love to," Raymond said. His enthusiasm sounded even more sincere.

"Good, I'm going to go tell Leo."

After Tracy John left the room, I asked, "What was all that about?"

"Why don't you tell me, Maine?"

"You don't want to get stuck out on some lake with them. They use worms as bait. Real worms."

"I'm not afraid of real worms."

"You aren't?"

"No."

"You don't want to go fishing. You don't even eat fish."

"Like I said, I would love to go fishing, Maine."

"You're going to be bored out of your mind, stuck out there all day."

"You know that for a fact?"

"You're not exactly the manly rugged type."

"What are you trying to say?" Raymond asked, lapsing into his Mr. Hyde demeanor.

"You're not the manly rugged type," I repeated.

"I'm putting my foot down," he said heatedly.

"You can put whatever you want down, Raymond," I told him.

He rose to his feet. "All my life people have put me in

a box. I didn't grow up with people who do things like fish, but that doesn't mean I've never wanted to. You've put me in a cardboard box, and you're hung up on that—that—that clown!"

"You don't make sense. How is this about Demetrius? Tracy John would never ask Demetrius to go fishing with him. Tracy John doesn't even like Demetrius."

"Tracy John is an excellent judge of character," he said as he went to the door.

"Where are you going?" I asked him.

His parting words were: "I'm not going to stay in a cardboard box, Maine."

Men . . . Having brothers, a boy cousin, Daddy, and uncles in my life, you would think I would have a clear understanding of them. But I didn't even comprehend women, and I am one.

Later that evening, Leo tried to break it down for me.

"You shouldn't have said he wasn't rugged. That's like calling him a sissy," Leo told me.

"I never called him a sissy."

"I said it was *like* calling him a sissy, Maine. Don't you get it? There are certain things you can't do if you are a guy."

I scratched through my thick Afro to get to my scalp. "What can't you do as a male?"

"Like, act polite like he does."

"Oh, Leo, please."

"And walk around with books like he does."

"How are books feminine? Most are written by men. In some countries, women are forbidden to read."

"You still don't understand. Look, I take dance lessons."

"No kidding, Leo."

"People say things after that."

"Like what?"

"Things."

"Things like, 'You're a good dancer.'"

Leo shook his head and said, "It's just hard. . . ."

More cryptic gobbledygook. I swear, sometimes I think the world decides to become unglued all at once. What was I supposed to do, lie to my boyfriend and tell him he was a he-man? Everybody was so touchy. I'd have to re-member to ask my friend Cissy to find out if she ever minded being called a sissy.

Along this same theme, I overheard Daddy and Tracy John in the living room later that evening.

"When Uppercase E got to be about Leo's age, he started to turn. It's all right to be smart when you're little and make like you want to learn, but as you get older, it's tough. And Escalus used to love to sing in the choir, both school and church. But it got tougher to show that side of himself. Uppercase E changed overnight. Next time I looked around, he was going in a totally different direc-tion. I barely recognized him."

"What did he look like, Unc?" Tracy John asked.

"Well, one day he came walking in the house in a snakeskin jacket."

Tracy John's mouth flew open; then he asked, "What kind of snakes?"

"Green ones. Pretty soon, everything was going wrong. Uppercase E was no dummy, but he started having trouble in school and fell in with the wrong crowd."

I got closer to the door frame. This was, after all, the crucial part. I wanted to hear more about Uncle E's leap from choirboy to criminal.

"Some mighty terrible things happen when you stop being yourself," Daddy told Tracy John.

"I'm glad Uncle E's not on the lam no more. I can't wait till we all go fishing. It's great to have him here." Tracy John sounded so happy, it touched my heart.

"One thing's for sure, Tracy John, everybody needs a home."

Awwwww. In fact, double awwwww. Though I didn't get the answers I wanted, eavesdropping on the two of them was better than watching *The Wonderful World of Disney*. Plus, it really made me think, not so much about Uncle E as about Raymond.

I didn't want Raymond to get caught up in a world of crime, so the next day I planned to tell him he was an alpha male. That was my intention, but as soon as I saw him in the hall, he gave me a look that was so frosty, I decided to return the favor. Then he outright scowled at me, and I grimaced back at him. I know this sounds immature of me, but he started it. I jettisoned the idea of stroking Raymond's bruised ego.

During English class, we sat as if royalty on thrones, side by side.

Our words went out, but not between us. I made up my mind right then and there: I didn't need him as a boyfriend, and I felt immediately relieved to be free of his funky old paranoid schizophrenic attitude.

sixteen

My older brother, Horace, wrote from time to time, updating us on how much he was taking advantage of the island hospitality. He hadn't dispatched pictures of himself in his uniform in a while. Instead, the last photo he forwarded to us was of him in a natty Hawaiian shirt and groovy shorts, sipping a tropical drink decorated with pineapple pieces. In that shot, he was flanked by two local girls. They had wide noses, full lips, innocent faces, long, glossy black hair, and curvy but toned bodies. I flipped the photo over and saw that Horace had penned the words *God Bless America.*

In the accompanying letter, PV2 Upshaw went on about how sick he was of the mess hall food. He also bemoaned Hawaii's lack of seasons, describing the very little weather variations as "terminally beautiful." He told us that occasionally a volcano erupted.

The bulk of the correspondence was dedicated to Uncle E, but Horace closed with a postscript, some long-distance humor, just for me: "Daddy told me that you want to go Hollywood. I can't believe my humble little sister has dreams of seeing her name in lights. I want to make sure, Maine, your newfound success doesn't go to your head, but seeing as this letter won't reach you for a week, I'm probably too late."

That evening, Daddy, Tracy John, and I went to pick up Uncle E from work at the discount furniture store on Fifty-second Street. It was a crawl of linked rooms. Tracy John took a left as Daddy went right. I followed my cousin, only to find him jumping on a display bed. With one scoop I pulled him down, and we continued toward the back of the store.

We passed by a red crushed-velour chaise, and he stopped again.

"What kind of sofa is that?" Tracy John asked.

"It's a fainting couch."

Tracy John gave me a quizzical look.

"You don't know what fainting is?"

He shook his head. I moved him to the side and demonstrated, pretending like I was receiving some shocking news. "What! In the year 1996, Tracy John gives up his position on the Dallas Cowboys to play baseball for the Philadelphia Phillies?" Then I held the back of my hand to my forehead and dissolved into the fall. I made sure the chaise was safely beneath me as I guided myself down.

Next Tracy John gave it a try. "What! Maine is going to play for the Dallas Cowboys?" He got the shocking news part right, but he did too much of a direct drop.

I offered this critique: "It's got to be more of a surrender, as if you really blacked out."

"How do you wake them up?" he asked, still in character, lying on the chaise with his eyes closed.

"You're going to need a bucket of water."

His eyes opened. He seemed really interested in that.

"Ice cold," I told him. "And you dump it over their heads."

He sat up and told me, "I want to try it again."

He did, and he was still too robotic. It surprised me that such a natural athlete was so stiff.

"Sometimes you can do a twirl like this." I demonstrated what I meant.

Imitating me, Tracy John spun like a top.

Just then, a salesman came by asking an ominous "May I help you?"

This store didn't take the plastic covers off their furniture, so we weren't harming anything, but still, I grabbed Tracy John's hand, and we went where we were supposed to be. Around in the back of the store, I heard a gravelly voice say, "All right, we lift on three.... One...two... and three."

There were two thickset men with blunt hands, a more

sinewy Uncle E, and a happy medium, muscular Daddy (Daddy was always helping out), all hefting a massive rolltop desk. This thing was as big as a baby grand piano.

My eyes stayed fastened to my uncle. He seemed to have the same amount of sweat on his brow as the other guys. Was he really reformed? Once the desk was off the truck and on the showroom floor, Uncle E punched out.

Later that night, Tracy John and I practiced fainting some more. Leo got into the act and, of course, with all his dance training, was able to show both Tracy John and me up. What form! What grace! There was no contest. Leo was the best fake fainter in the house.

Too bad there was no call for it. Guys never faint in movies.

seventeen

Not having Raymond to receive calls from left my evenings free. I read more of *The Pearl*. I had gotten to the point where the main character, Kino, found the gigantic pearl, and he was happy that finally he'd be financially set. However, his wife was against the oversized jewel. She claimed that it was haunted, so he bopped her one. I mean, he really let her have it. At that point, I stopped reading in sequence and flipped ahead to the later parts of the book.

Kino's wife was in it till the end, so somehow they patched things up. What kind of message is that? I was completely appalled that Mr. Mand would assign such an anti–women's lib book. This was 1976, after all.

I hated Kino and vowed he'd never get me back on his bandwagon. I wished the author had shown him as a rat from the beginning, not as a caring husband. I felt tricked and cheated and decided that even though Steinbeck was sympathetic to the indigenous population of Mexico, he'd lost me as a fan.

As luck would have it, in class the next day, almost as soon as my behind hit the seat, the teacher called on me.

"I'm sorry, Mr. Mand, I haven't gotten that far in the book," I confessed.

A stunned look swept over his face.

Behind me, I heard the class stir. What hypocrites! For years, I'd witnessed my classmates scribbling down notes after I spoke. Lots of people came to class without doing the assignment; I would guess the majority of them didn't. They sat back very comfortably. Daddy always said many hands make light work, so it was ironic that on the one day I refused to be the Rosa Parks of my English class, this one time that I came to school unprepared, the whole world collapsed.

Raymond didn't let his end drop, and he bantered on about poor Kino, the pearl fisherman, and how the capitalist system changed him into a monster.

"I'm not convinced that communism is such a bad idea," Mr. Mand mused aloud.

I wasn't sure Mr. Mand was red, but he was at the very least pink, and I wasn't referring to his peaches-and-cream complexion. That snapped me back into things. Communism wasn't so bad? Around the world, most recently in Cambodia, millions had died under its banner.

"Please try to finish the fourth chapter," Mr. Mand instructed. He seemed to look directly at me.

I nodded uneasily and looked over at Raymond.

The buzzer buzzed.

Raymond said this dig before walking out: "I think Demetrius is rubbing off on you."

eighteen

That did it. What a creep, I thought. I hate when people jump to conclusions. I was mad practically the whole day, but then at school's dismissal, my heart melted and my anger faded.

It used to be that he would catch up with me after school, but now there was no wide grin to greet me. There was nothing. What's that saying about never missing water until the well is dry? That afternoon, I figured I might as well give Raymond a chance to apologize to me. I called and called. It rang and rang. Too bad his household was so tiny. If only he'd had meddling siblings, I would have cracked through a lot easier.

I did better after his folks came home. "Hi, Mr. Newell. Is Raymond there?" I asked, and didn't notice that I was clutching the receiver in both hands.

"He just stepped into the shower, Charmaine."

That's bull, I thought, but I'd never say that to Mr. Newell. Who takes a shower at six-thirty in the evening? "Well, thank you. If you could just leave the message. 'Maine called. Call her back.' You know, when he can."

"Of course, Charmaine."

And of course, I didn't hear from him that evening.

When I went downstairs, I found out that everything had been taken over by Uncle E. He'd been working a lot, and I'd been going to sleep earlier, not catching his late show.

Uncle E quarterbacked and kept the group from straying by singing lead and keeping the melody on his guitar. One of Daddy's pinochle friends had a washboard. (I bet he took it from his wife's laundry basket.) However he learned such a skill, he was on beat. Leo and Tracy John shared bongo duty. Daddy breathed in and out of a harmonica. Those two thick-necked guys from the furniture store made the best of simple instruments; they played the spoons.

Oh, my God, I thought, this is what people were forced to do before there was TV. There they were in the living room; I wouldn't get to see a show for the rest of the night.

Another one of Daddy's friends, who always wore a kofi, remarkably kept it straight and square on his head as he played bass. And who knew Daddy knew someone who played the violin—sorry, the fiddle? (Why do fiddlers have to stamp their feet when they play?)

I was trying to decipher their song but couldn't. It

sounded country, quite a feat because as far as I knew, the Upshaw side of the family hadn't worked on a farm since 1865. Daddy always talked about "in the country," despite the fact that he grew up in West Philly, a place not known for its wide-open spaces. I could conceive of this if it were from Ma's people from way down in Alabama. It would be understandable if *they* would wax about lean stalks of field cane.

They had a real hoedown going on, singing lines like "All right now" and "Hey, hey" and "Put your hands together" and "That's all right" and "Yeah" and "Uh-huh" and just plain "Sing it."

All these ad-libs hyped up and punctuated the song. At the end, or should I say just when I thought it was over, someone yelled, "One more time!"

A voice inside me screamed *Get out of there, Maine, before someone hands you a tambourine!*

nineteen

Leo had dance and Tracy John was over at Basil's and Ma had gone to the fruit truck for some bananas (we were having pudding that night). It was now or never. I stole up to the attic in the hopes of finding out just who Uncle E was once and for all.

I wanted to find something incriminating to finally rip the wool off my family's eyes. This was the man who got caught with a nickel bag, after all.

Fell in with the wrong crowd, my heinie. I took the steps two at a time.

Sure he'd make out like he was working so hard moving furniture, and make like he was so gentle, with his guitar and everything, but I knew. . . . I knew there was something up here, a stash of some kind of stolen items or drugs. (Would I even know what angel dust looks like? Did it look like regular dust?) Or a roach clip? (Whatever did *that* look like?) As Charmaine Upshaw, P.I., I hoped that if I found a gun, it would have a safety on it, though I didn't know what that switch looked like either. I had to find some vice.

Be fearless, I kept telling myself, though I was tortured by the thought that I might prick myself with a junkie's needle, then get some sort of infection and wake up later that night with a raging fever. Curiosity kills, indeed.

In my detective work, I left no article of underwear un-turned. But I didn't find any illicit material, just cough drops (got to keep that voice smooth).

At last I uncovered something, a black book. I imag-ined a listing of crimes. I flipped the book over and was disappointed. All that damn digging and all I found was a Holy Bible.

I leafed through the pages and a few letters eased out. I picked one up:

Dear Baby Sis:

Or should I say, "Momma." Congratulations! This is wonderful news! It's the best news in the world. You will be a great mother, and you will have a beautiful little girl or handsome boy or both— remember Pop was a twin. Something tells me that you will have a girl, though; I can just feel it through the miles. Whichever, she or he will be a fine upstanding person that everyone will be proud of, just like you. Everybody makes mistakes—I understand that better than most. You did the right thing; you got yourself free. You didn't wait for the red light to flash over and over; you left. He's a very, very sick man, and I'm so proud of you for wriggling free before you really got hurt. He reminds me of some of the folks in here. All ego and as fragile as an egg. They never go for a fair fight; they like sneak attacks. But that's all behind you now, Karyn. I could go on and say, "Keep your head up," but you always land on your feet. You'll be a nurse soon, and you have a host of friends, and I suspect it won't be long before you find some other guy who loves and cares for you and your baby. As you know, we're not all bad. I'll close as always, saying I wish I could be there to help. I know that's what I always say, but time is so weird here. Some days go on forever and other days fly by. Often it seems like you and Peyton and Otis and Ma and Pop are so close. I guess that's what comes from growing up with people—even when you're gone from sight, you're never gone from my mind or heart. Don't spend one second worrying about me, Karyn. You got out of your prison, one day I'll have the sense to get out of mine.

All my love to you and my soon-to-be-born niece or nephew,

Yours, Escalus

Though there were other letters, I read this one repeatedly. As I did, it was like the planet shifted an inch or two. It was all so clear to me now. Uncle E didn't have anything up his sleeves; he simply missed his family and wanted to see us again.

How much neater things would have been if I'd found a boogeyman. Wouldn't it be easier if Uncle E was unreformed and packing or dealing?

Like smoke up a chimney, my feelings of disdain dissipated. But what would replace them?

So this was the real Escalus Upshaw: a guitar in the corner, slacks in the bottom drawer, and on top, underwear where my underwear used to be and letters to his little sister.

There was no monster.

"Charmaine," a voice downstairs called. I quickly put everything back where it was.

I tore down two flights and said, "Hi, Ma, just back from the fruit stand?" I sounded abnormal, even for me.

Ma popped me an odd look, but I was used to that.

Later, when Uncle E got home, I cracked a grin his way as we passed each other in the hall. He returned the expression, but I wasn't sure he noticed the difference in me.

What I wanted to say was *What's a grand between family members?* but those were words I knew I'd never be able to utter. As tall as I was, I still wasn't big enough.

twenty

The sky was white-gray, and I wondered when spring would get here. I hoped it wouldn't rain on Tracy John's first baseball game. Their uniforms were blue and yellow and baggy like the old-fashioned players' from the twenties.

During the warm-up, the team members tossed the ball around while the stands filled.

When I turned to Ma to make a comment, I saw she was dabbing her eyes.

"Ma, don't," I warned.

The tears came down harder.

"Don't, Ma."

She fished in her purse for a new tissue.

"Ma, everyone is looking at us."

She cried, "It seems like only yesterday."

"What seems like only yesterday?"

"He was so young."

I did a double take at Tracy John and then a triple take at Ma. "He looks the same age he did yesterday."

"He's growing up right before us" was all she was able to get out before more trickles came from her eyes.

Next thing I knew, Tracy John came off the field. "What's wrong, Auntie?" he asked.

She touched his face lightly. "Nothing's wrong."

I glanced about us. Before, I was just talking, but now I could tell—people were staring.

Basil waved at Tracy John, and the coach blew his whistle for him to return to the field.

Just then, Uncle E strolled up.

"Uncle E, you made it!" Tracy John cheered.

Uncle E opened up his arms and gave his nephew a big hug. "I promised you I would. Now go out there and do your stuff."

Tracy John stormed the field. After the game was under way, Uncle E placed his hand on Ma's knee.

"Lela Mae, you got to let him go," he told my mother. "I know it's not easy, but you got to let him go."

Suddenly, Ma managed to collect herself.

Even without his magic guitar, Uncle E had a magic quality.

As we watched the game, it occurred to me that my little cousin wasn't getting old. Who was Ma kidding? Everyone was young that day.

A fly ball was hit out in center field, and Tracy John got right underneath it, bracing it with the other hand so it wouldn't fall.

There was a chant of "Go, Dardon, go." People had their arms up, pumping hard. Tracy John took his glove off and his friends high-fived each other.

Uncle E, Ma, and I stood up and clapped. Uncle E leaned into me and said, "He's following right in his mother's footsteps. You know, her team went all the way to the state championship."

"Really?" I asked.

He nodded.

This time we shared a real smile. He did have a nice smile. It was like Daddy's, wide—it lifted his whole face.

In the fifth inning, Tracy John got a base hit, but there were already two outs and the next player on his team fouled.

Game over, as this was Little League and we were cheated out of a few innings.

"My mommy made it all the way to the finals?" Tracy John asked. He still had his loose-hanging uniform on when he came to the table.

"We saw it with our own eyes," Uncle E told us over dinner.

"Those West Philly girls were playing some ball that day," Daddy said. "Did you tell him the best part?"

"No, you tell him, Peyton," Uncle E told Daddy.

"You go on and say it," Daddy said.

"Will somebody tell me!" Tracy John asked.

"Well, I nearly fell out the stands when I saw Karyn hit that home run," Uncle E said.

"Get out!" Tracy John exclaimed as if he'd just received the shock of his life.

"Uppercase E is serious, Tracy John," Daddy said.

"Was it a girl home run or a regular one?" my cousin asked.

I smiled. Auntie Karyn would be tickled by her son's question.

Uncle E went on to explain that it was by no means a "girl home run," it was a legit one. It had nothing to do with anyone being afraid to run for the ball; the ball actually traveled over the fence.

Tracy John's eyes sparkled when he heard that.

"I remember it like it was yesterday. She swung and did her usual hustle, but by the time she left first, she could tell she had it, and she broke into what they call the second-base trot."

I could imagine the great amphitheater of the grandstand. The crowd buzzing while the vendors hawked their wares. Everyone going wild with excitement. All shouting our family name—"Upshaw! Upshaw! Upshaw!"

"I've seen that," Leo said. "That's what Hank Aaron does. Once he knows he has it, he jogs and waves till he gets back home."

"She did that?" Tracy John turned to Daddy and Uncle E.

"You better believe it," Uncle E said.

twenty-one

I still had Raymond's book, which gave me hope. Not so much about finding my way to the silver screen, but I held on to the aspiration that Raymond would one day break down and ask for his book back. As one day tripped into another, it dawned on me that that time might not be soon. It might be years from now, way in the future, like 1993 or something. Someday, he'd long for the way he kissed my palm. He'd pine for me.

In the meantime, I passed some time going through the curious case of Peg Entwistle. Who, you ask? Exactly. In the 1930s, she committed suicide by leaping from the Hollywood sign. The book said she had gotten some work, but only small parts. Since she couldn't be "somebody," she chose to be nobody. Imagine the determination that took. I bet if she'd hung around a little longer, she could have channeled that ambition and become an astronaut.

Instead she chose to jump from the *H*. And why not jump off one of the *L*s? Why not the *Y*? I'd never studied the topic of suicide, but from my layman's knowledge, I surmised that people don't really want to kill themselves. They just want to be that H-word—happy. In symbolism, everything can be explained as a front for something else. But since the meaning of this woman's act was so facile, I had other questions:

First, how did this untrained woman get all the way up there? Did she have scaling apparatus or hiking boots? Did she bring a ladder?

Second, didn't she attract attention? Where was security? And if there were no night watchmen guarding this world-famous landmark, whose bright idea was that?

Third, what was she wearing during this, her final act? I knew it didn't get that cold in California, but I would think she'd at least have had a jacket draped about her shoulders. Underneath, I bet she had one of those beaded evening gowns. Maybe it was mauve colored, or a softer shade. Was it strapless? Or, my favorite, one-shouldered?

The real tragedy was that she wasn't famous for the *why* of her suicide, but for the *how*. As far as suicidal people go, I guess, I don't empathize either way. I consider all the people in hospitals fighting off diseases, and I dwell on all the starving children in the world, but most of all I think of beautiful, wonderful Auntie Karyn. Not only was she an aunt but she was a mother, sister, daughter, friend, nurse, honor student, award-winning essayist, community activist, and (as I'd learned as of late) champion softball player. She would have been twenty-seven now, twenty-eight on June 12 if she hadn't been taken. And I got so angry at Peg Entwistle. I was as angry at her as I was at that imaginary Kino for hitting his imaginary wife.

Tearing up, I smeared the ink that told of Entwistle. Anyone looking at the book after me would think her story moved me that much.

The moon hung between two heavy clouds. I wanted to stay up late. All night if I had to, just to get something else but dislike in my brain.

Then the phone rang, and I waited suspended in air, as I thought, Let it be for me.

"Maine, it's for you," Leo told me.

Thinking it was Raymond or Millicent or Cissy, I jumped three feet off the floor.

"Charmaine Upshaw, this is a reminder call from the Thomas Sharpe Talent Agency. Classes will be starting soon. Register now to avoid disappointment."

"Oh, yes. I'm so looking forward—" I rushed to say, but then realized I wasn't talking to anyone. It was a recorded message. I'd been called by a robot. What would they think of next?

twenty-two

Wouldn't you know it? Almost to the second that I started liking Uncle E, I came to find out his days of freedom were numbered. No wonder Daddy had said he only needed a few weeks to stay in our house. I guess it was as good an idea as any: to stockpile some honest money before you go into the slammer so when you finally do get out, you have some change rattling in your pocket and you are less likely to be tempted back into street life. Plus, there was the added bonus of hanging out with your kinfolk for a spell. I could understand keeping all this from little Tracy John, but I should have been in the adult loop. Everything happened so quickly. On the day he was to turn himself in for the original charge that he'd skipped out on back in October of last year, I saw Uncle E, surrounded and all suited up. I couldn't pretend that I understood all the intricacies of law enforcement, but I thought of how much life is like a movie that you walk in on in the middle of. You never quite figure out what exactly has gone on before.

A breeze sent a shiver down my spine. Don't send him away now, I thought. I used to think he was a jerk but now I see he's all right.

Of course, Tracy John threw a fit, asking why couldn't he go with Uncle E to court.

Ma kept telling him, "That's strictly for grown-ups, Tracy John."

A lot of people would be there: Daddy, of course, Gammy, Uncle O. Along with a host of character witnesses from the furniture store.

And a lot of people from church.

"Even the rev?" Tracy John asked.

Ma nodded. "Reverend Clee cares about his flock."

Suddenly, Tracy John became more relaxed. He even took on an assured air. "Oh, then we got this one."

"The Scriptures say 'Thy will be done,'" I said, not so much to cool his confidence as to keep him realistic.

"Nope," Tracy John said.

I looked at him skeptically and asked, "They don't say that?"

He shook his head.

"What do they say, then?"

He pointed to himself with his thumb. "My will be done."

I shook my head and told him to quit messing around with statements like that, before he incurred the wrath.

Everyone would say, "He was such a cute kid before he got struck by lightning."

Mid-evening, we heard Daddy try the back door. We all went to greet what we thought would be them, but he was alone. His eyes swept the room, then lowered a little, and he shook his head to signify that the news was not good.

Ma's lips parted in shock. Leo and Tracy John said things like "How?" and "Why?"

My lips pursed—I was annoyed. God, I thought. You really are a comedian. You really know how to keep your jokes coming.

"Listen, we live in this country, and we have to follow its rules. We're all gonna miss him, but he didn't get life. He'll be out in ninety days."

"That's three months," Leo said.

Tracy John counted on his fingers. "March, April, May. That means he won't be back until June."

Daddy nodded.

"We're supposed to go fishing next weekend."

"I know, Tracy John, I know," Daddy said. "We can all go when he gets out."

"June is too long to wait, Unc."

Tracy John's words seemed to bounce about the room. He stamped his foot. "Three months is a long time."

"Now, this is not the outcome we wanted," Daddy began, and in that moment he was the master of understatement. "But we will make it through this. And so will Escalus."

"I bet that judge wouldn't like it if someone put him in jail," Tracy John said.

Daddy's eyes bored into him. "Uppercase E couldn't have stayed out of trouble the best he could. The judge has to follow the law, Tracy John. That is his job. We'll make the best of things."

"Doesn't the judge know that was a long time ago? Uncle E isn't like that anymore. He was working at the furniture store. He was playing the guitar. He wasn't hurting anyone," Tracy John said.

"We can't solve every problem in the universe tonight, Tracy John," Daddy finally said.

"Uncle E never hurt anyone," Tracy John repeated.

Daddy went back to giving him no answer. Then my cousin made the statement: "I bet he wouldn't have to go to jail if he was white."

Where did that come from? Just a few months ago, Tracy John was in this very same room asking, "What's racism?" How much of the world could he have absorbed since then, to put together things like this? If Escalus Upshaw was white with steel gray, no, pastel blue eyes, a granite chin, and an aquiline nose, would his fate have been the same?

"What color is your uncle E?"

Tracy John looked stunned, as if Daddy was asking him a trick question.

He looked to his right, where I was standing. I was just as paralyzed by the inquiry.

"What color is Uncle E?" Daddy repeated.

Tracy John looked around again. "My uncle E?"

"Yes. Yes," Daddy said. "Your uncle E."

Tracy John swallowed and finally offered a tentative "Black?"

"Exactly." Daddy paused to let that set in. Then he said in his big, round voice, "It is a waste of time to suppose what would happen if he wasn't. We have to live in reality. Let's not give white people too much credit. Even if the judge was a racist, two wrongs don't make a right. But two Wrights did make an airplane."

He had used that pun before, usually to more positive response. This time there was not even a chuckle. Tough crowd.

Daddy told Tracy John, "Now, you, to bed."

"But it's not even seven o'clock."

Daddy didn't speak, just pointed upstairs with his thumb, and Ma quickly ushered him away.

Up until that moment, Daddy had been one cool customer, but the look on his face now that Tracy John was out of the room was that of a totally broken man. He pulled out a chair and crumpled into it like a worn-out paper bag. He said one word. "Damn."

The next morning, Ma fixed oatmeal, the blandest food ever created. Despite this sedating food, everything erupted again when Tracy John asked how soon we would be going to go see Uncle E.

Daddy blew in his bowl and informed him that Uncle E would not be receiving us as visitors.

Tracy John let out a flurry of "Why not?"s and "How come?"s, then finally a "Please."

Daddy's voice boomed over Tracy John's. "We can write him a letter."

There are people who hold things in and let them fester and fester and then develop an ulcer. I was convinced that Tracy John would never have to worry about that. He sprang to his feet in protest. "A letter!"

Daddy shot him a look. "You got a problem with letters?"

Tracy John retreated, sinking back into the chair. I felt a light sweat break out on my neck.

"No, I don't have a problem with letters."

"Now, we all have to get ahold of ourselves. This is not the end of anything. This is just a slight detour. We will do him like we do Horace," Daddy said—what amounted in sports movies to the pep talk. When your team is behind, that's the time to talk about apple pie and the flag.

The team was not inspired.

Daddy pointed to Tracy John. "And you?"

"Yes?" Reluctantly and mournfully, Tracy John looked Daddy's way.

Daddy held his chin in his hand and gave him two words of instruction: "Cheer up."

twenty-three

"Struggle is a part of life. Struggle is life," Reverend Clee told his congregation.

"Yes, Lord," Mrs. Langley said.

"We struggle to come into being. That is called birth."

Mr. Brown raised one hand. "All right now."

"Then after we're born, we struggle to make the most of our lives."

Someone gave a stray "Hallelujah."

"We struggle to get along with friends and find someone special to share our lives with."

"Amen," I said, since that one hit a soft spot with me.

"We struggle to make the most of our lives with that special someone."

Like a lab rat on a spinning wheel, round and round we go, that was the gist of Reverend Clee's sermon that Sunday.

"Never expect not to struggle," the rev told us.

I glanced over at Tracy John. He gave our rev a glacial stare.

I nudged him. "What's the matter?"

He shot me a dirty look.

As we exited and threaded through the crowd, the rev held his customary spot by the door. He shook hands with the members.

Tracy John tried to ease by without the rev's notice, but he was halted.

"What is the rush, Tracy John, and why the long face?"

"I didn't like your sermon," Tracy John said.

"You didn't?" the rev asked.

"No, I didn't," Tracy John said. "I don't like struggle."

I fell back in a swoon. By the time I regained my bearings, Tracy John had vanished. I had to hand it to him, he knew where to disappear to, right into a nest of women. When I found him, he was getting his right cheek pinched by one of them. When he saw me, he quickly gave me his fang face.

Later at home, when I attempted to confront Tracy John on his behavior, he pointed his finger at me. "You have always been against Uncle E."

"How do you know what I've always been?" I asked.

He humphed. "I know you want your room back. You're glad Uncle E's in jail."

"That is a horrible thing to say, Tracy John. Do you think that little of me?"

Tracy John looked away, frowning.

I shook my head. "You carrying on like this will not make things better. Uncle E will be all right."

He turned to me with his brows raised. "You don't know that for sure."

"There's no need worrying now if nothing has happened."

"Something has happened." His voice rose too. "He's in jail!"

"You know what I mean, Tracy John."

"You know what *I* mean, Maine."

And he characteristically stormed from the room. Forget about Hollywood, Tracy John had the temperament of a male diva. He belonged in the Metropolitan Opera. This is something no one ever brings up: How the family of a jailed person suffers. The toll that it took in legal costs was nothing compared to this emotional burden. The limbo state that everyone was suddenly in. The mystery, the uncertainty. Tracy John had cause to be worried. Anything could happen in the big house.

Before Tracy John turned in for the night, I gave it one more try. I hung by his door with paper and a pencil and asked him the straightforward question, "Want to write a letter?"

"No," Tracy John said flatly.

"How is he going to hear from you, then?"

"He should have never turned himself in, Maine. At least then he'd be free."

"What kind of freedom is that, Tracy John? Constantly moving. Nobody wants that. Remember what a wise man once told you: Everybody needs a home."

That made him look even sadder, so I told him, "I think you've got this thing all wrong. Uncle E's one lucky man."

"Say what!"

"He's lucky to have a nephew who cares about him so much. Back in January when Daddy first told us he needed our help, you were the first one to volunteer. You have such a good heart, Tracy John. I know you are not going to let all these months go by without so much as a word."

Soon we were sitting at his desk, composing words for our uncle. When we were done, Tracy John held the stamp out to me. "Lick this."

"What's wrong with your tongue?" I asked him.

He said he didn't like the taste. I didn't know why that was. Stamps were, to me, sweet. Still, there was room for postal improvement. If you moistened the postage too much or not enough, it would come off. Couldn't somebody someday invent self-adhesive stamps?

I was just about to seal the envelope when he said, "Not yet."

"Why not?"

He told me he wanted to include a sentence tomorrow about how the practice went.

De-liver De-letter De-sooner De-better. I timed it just right. I arrived at the end of practice.

"Did you forget to bring it?" Tracy John asked, seeing nothing in my hands.

I played dumb. "Bring what?"

Then I pulled the letter out of my bag and handed it to him so he could write the coda. I looked over his shoulder. He would have been an excellent cub reporter, determined to get every last detail.

"Come on, come on, hurry." He took off like lightning, dragging me by the hand behind him.

Of course, we couldn't simply put it in the mailbox. We had to take it to that redbrick building on Church Lane. (I couldn't convince him that since Dardon was so small, it really didn't matter, the post office wouldn't get it out any sooner.)

Dardon's P.O. was, as far as I could tell, a one-man operation. Maybe there were tons of people in the back, milling about, but front and center it was always this one fellow with sandy, close-cut hair and a thin face.

"Can you put this letter on the top of your pile, so it will get there faster?" Tracy John asked.

The man took one look at my cousin, then at the letter (obviously noting its penal colony address), then back at Tracy John. He smiled and said, "Sure thing."

Just as we were leaving, we passed the America's Most Wanted posting. I wondered why the FBI chose to hang their faces here. But then I thought, Even fugitives from justice have to buy stamps eventually. For the first time, I peered at their mugs and felt a twinge of sympathy. They could be somebody's uncle.

"Wait a minute, I forgot to do something," Tracy John said, and ran back to the window. He pointed at the pile and the postman fished the letter out for him.

Tracy John put the letter to his chest and then held it up to the ceiling. After he said a silent chant, he gave it back to the mailman.

"You can't tell or else it won't come true," the postman told him.

"I know that," Tracy John replied.

I imagined Uncle E in the yard during mail call, a smile creeping onto his face.

Next Sunday service, Tracy John was much better behaved.

He even had an apology for Reverend Clee. "I'm sorry I said I didn't like your sermon."

The rev reeled Tracy John in for a good hug.

"That's all right, young man. I know how we get at times like this. We are an emotional people."

"That's for sure," I said, patting my cousin's head.

Just then Ma and Daddy came and stood behind Tracy John.

The rev told him, "Don't you fret about your uncle E. God will look out for him. He rescued Daniel from the lions' den. He parted the Red Sea for Moses. He helped Samson beat all those Philistines—"

Tracy John smiled broadly and interrupted, "With the jawbone of an ass."

Ma's "Say 'donkey,' sweetheart" collided with Daddy's "Our boy sure knows the Bible."

twenty-four

At the start of chemistry class, Mr. Mirabelle asked someone to pull down the shades and someone else to turn the lights off. Were we going to watch a movie in science class? Now, that was a first. Not that I was complaining. Anything would be a lot more intriguing than those molecular configurations he usually drew on the board.

Mr. Mirabelle manned the projector, and we proceeded to watch the show.

It was one of those old Duck and Cover movies from way back in the 1950s, when the girls wore crinolines and floppy ponytails. It featured lamebrain survival tactics about how to deal with a catastrophic explosion, such as: "Have a good flashlight on hand—the electricity might go out." This crapola was produced by the Federal Civil Defense Administration, an organization that by the seventies, I hoped, would have been laughed out of operation.

The film only lasted fifteen minutes, and when it was over Mr. Mirabelle flipped on the lights. He wanted us to recite the terms we had heard in the movie.

I was all set to say "gamma rays" when someone blurted out, "How come no blacks were in that movie?"

Mr. Mirabelle's droopy eyes lifted in surprise.

I admit that question threw me, for I hadn't noticed that that black-and-white movie had an all-white cast. But unlike the underrepresentation of us in that modeling slide show I'd attended, I didn't get up in arms over this. Studies have shown that civilization began in Africa. Maybe it's enough of a claim to fame to be the first people on earth. I guess we don't have to be the last.

"Didn't they want us to survive the blast?" someone else asked.

Even Demetrius chimed in "Yeah," but I had the feeling that on his part it wasn't righteous indignation, it was the fear that Mr. Mirabelle would actually get back to teaching chemistry.

You would think we'd been watching *Birth of a Nation*, the way the class was so worked up. I'd never seen Mr. Mirabelle wearing the proverbial deer-in-the-headlights look. He was a man of science, and the absence of black faces in these movies was something that had never even occurred to him—much the way "blackness" hadn't been thought of by the inventor of "flesh"-colored bandages, or by the genius at Crayola who decided to call one of the sixty-four colors "flesh." It was so weird to see this epiphany wash over his face, as if to say *You know, I never looked at it that way.*

As I walked home, I wished Raymond had shared that class with me. He'd have been a great person to offer insight. I thought of phoning him to ask if there was ever a bomb shelter movie from a brother's perspective—perhaps Oscar Micheaux had been commissioned or something. But deep down I knew I couldn't contact my ex-boyfriend. It would be too awkward. No one calls out of the clear blue sky to talk about nuclear war.

When I got home I asked Ma, "How come you never told me about the bomb?"

"Charmaine, what are you talking about?" she asked me, and promptly put me to work. Before I knew it, I was working the rolling pin. She said we were having apple sour cream pie, which sounded way complicated. Luckily, all I had to do was the shell.

I pinched the dough around the pan to make a high crust. "Do you know about gamma rays?"

"Child, I wish you'd stop talking about that around this food. You're liable to contaminate the whole kitchen."

Her comment really got me imagining life in a bomb shelter. The movie said to be sure to have a wide assortment of canned foods on hand. With my luck, the can opener would probably break the first day. Even if it didn't, life would be so monotonous. I could picture Ma pacing and wringing her hands, slowly going stir-crazy after being robbed of her favorite hobby: cooking every day. And it's not like canned foods even come in a wide array. Any candied yams? Any black-eyed peas? Probably we'd have lousy tomato soup seven days week.

Of course, you shouldn't be picky at the end of the world. When the earth was beset by Armageddon, your perspective would naturally adjust.

And then there's also freeze-dried food, which wasn't mentioned in the movie. Horace told me that during basic training he was given MREs (Meals Ready to Eat). He said they came in plastic sacks and featured food that all he had to do was add water to (hot, preferably, but cold would do) and stir. Still, this sounded so gross. Can you imagine dry lumps that you wet into beef stew and flakes that turned into applesauce? For beverages, there was instant coffee or a cherry drink that stained your mouth an unnatural bright red color and made you look like a vampire.

The next day in chemistry class, nuclear destruction was still the topic, and the fallout continued. Initially, Mr. Mirabelle was able to get some questions on topics other than race. Someone asked, "How many people can fit in a bomb shelter?" That was the premise that had launched at least a thousand sci-fi stories, where the bad guy kicked people out, complaining that there wasn't enough air to hold everyone. How cruel to be thrown out and have the door slammed behind you. I know if my daddy were running a bomb shelter, he'd never do anything like that. In fact, he'd leave the door propped open, to help out any stragglers.

Mr. Mirabelle was happy to tell us about carbon monoxide (bad) and carbon dioxide (good), but then someone else raised his hand and we were back to talking about the lack of inclusion.

Finally, Mr. Mirabelle said the chances of a bomb striking were remote. "Nuclear annihilation was more of a possibility in October of 1962," he explained. "Back then we were in the throes of the Cold War. It was John F. Kennedy versus Nikita Khrushchev."

"Which one won?" someone in the back asked.

After class, by my locker, I felt someone tug my arm. I turned and beheld the megawatt smile of Demetrius McGee. He said, "Charmaine, you can come to my bomb shelter anytime."

I was broiled. As if I didn't have enough to worry about, what with my uncle in jail!

I'd thought Demetrius was low before, when he wanted me to do his homework. This term, he wanted to use me all over again—only this time it was to make his girlfriend jealous.

Dinah loomed in the background.

I took a deep breath and delivered what I hoped would be my farewell address to him. "I'm not going to be a part of your ploy to spice things up between you and Dinah. There was a time, not so long ago, that I was hungry for any morsel of attention you felt like tossing my way. But Demetrius, I mean this sincerely: If the end of the world ever happened and my choice was your bomb shelter or doom, I'd rather glow in the dark."

twenty-five

I stayed up until my eyes felt sandy, aimlessly paging through the movie star book, wondering what was on the hit parade that night.

But there was no show. Uncle E had been gone almost two weeks now, and with the silence, all I could do was strain my memory muscles. I strained so much, I was surprised I didn't get a hernia in my head.

Then it came. A musical dusting at first, it became as bright as stars and moved in sequence with the slow-moving branches of the tree that stood to the right of the house. The cynical side of me concluded it was probably best not to get too used to people. Nothing in life was certain, and all you were really left with was an image or a melody, a memory of what had been. But at least, I knew that Uncle E's voice and guitar playing were real and not some staged act. I placed the movie star book to the side and took out a letter that I had smuggled from Uncle E's room. I'd been rereading it since my uncle had been gone.

Hi, Uppercase E,

Hope you are well. I'm back home since the day finally came (I'd thought I'd be pregnant forever). I'm sure you've heard all this but he's seven pounds, nine ounces and that's perfect according to my medical books. He's adorable to look at, and thanks to our big brother he has two names. Peyton said just calling him Tracy would confuse people. I don't think my son looks like a girl baby at all, and as you can see from the enclosed photo he's bald. (Doesn't his picture make you smile? It certainly has that effect on me.) But Peyton got his way and he's named John, after Pop Pop. Peyton has been such a help to me these past few months, him and Lela Mae (what a nice lady). I wouldn't have been able to finish school without them. Speaking of school, are you still taking that composition class? I'm sure as smart as you are, you're breezing through it. I read about a guy who went all through college, then got his law degree behind bars. You don't have to go that far but whatever you can get done while you're there will definitely help. I know there will be a lot out here waiting for you. I'm taking Tracy John for his second outside walk, so we can drop this in the box. Be forewarned, I'm going to be off for the next five weeks, so you'll be hearing a lot from me.

Love,

Karyn and Tracy John (four days old!)

The next morning I woke up super-early so I could catch Daddy before he left for work.

"I've decided against showbiz, Daddy. You're right, that agency is pretty fishy. But even so, I don't want to be on the cover of some dumb magazine."

"But that's what you wanted."

"I thought so too, but now I don't. Is that okay?"

"Sure, as long as you're sure about it, Charmaine. You know, there are other places that'd be more legit."

"Skip it. Hollywood's not me. I'm of the people." I gave him a kiss on the cheek. "Thanks again for offering to pay for the lessons."

With that done, I went back upstairs, as I still had over an hour before I usually left for school.

No sooner had I shut my eyes than I heard Tracy John say, "So I guess I won't get my ten bikes."

I sat up in bed. I was the biggest eavesdropper in the house, but he was a close second. "I thought you wanted twenty bikes."

"You told me not to be greedy," he said. "Are you really going to give up on modeling forever and ever?"

I nodded. "I think I want to do other things with my life."

"Me too. That's why I've decided not to play football."

143

I put my hand to his head. "Are you feeling all right?" I asked him.

"I mean *just* play football. I want to play football *and* baseball."

There was a hunger that burned in his penny-colored eyes as he said it. But it wasn't a hunger for fame or glory. He wanted personal satisfaction. "I want to hit a home run like my mommy did. I want to hit the ball so it goes over the fence."

twenty-six

By now we had settled into a routine. (1) I'd go to meet Tracy John at the end of his practice, (2) he'd write a few finishing touches to the letter, (3) we'd both haul our behinds over to the Dardon post office, (4) Tracy John would do his ritual over the letter before releasing it, (5) he and I would leisurely walk home.

But Wednesday put an end to all that. As I opened the door to 614 Dardon Avenue, I heard two voices inside, one soft and Southern (Ma, obviously) and the other deeper and with melodic undertones (Uncle E!).

Seeing was believing. As we stepped inside, we both goggled at his lean frame and those sad eyes, which lifted when he saw us.

"Uncle E!" Tracy John rushed up to him in one of his tackles. It was like water rushing against rock.

Triple awwwww. If only cameras had been rolling right

then, this heartwarming scene could have been sent to the evening news to melt away all the usual doom-and-gloom reportage.

I stood a little back from the fanfare, glad on the inside.

"We just sent you a letter," Tracy John told him.

"Well, I better get on back there, then," Uncle E joked.

I looked over at Ma and saw her eyes well up. She could never hold her tears. As the reunion wore on, Uncle E kissed Tracy John on his forehead and Ma on the cheek and they all joined in a group hug. I wanted to get in on the act but held back. Uncle E caught me standing off to the side, and telepathically he seemed to say everything to me all at once. I guess I had done a lousy job all along hiding my mistrust of him, never joining in with his songs and even going so far as to ease out of a room when I found him in it. I guess that was pretty petty of me. Now that all the dust had settled and he was home free, I'd be a total hypocrite if I hugged all over him, trying to make out like I'd been in his corner all the while.

"Come on over here, Tall Girl," Uncle E said.

Who could refuse such an invitation? Certainly not me. I threw my arms out wide and included myself in the warmth of our family's huddle.

Though it had come clear to me that I would never make it in the world of glamour and high fashion, I found out Uncle E had been a model—a model prisoner. After only serving a sliver of his sentence, he'd been let out for good behavior.

On Sunday Reverend Clee gave a service in his honor. All the focus was on Uncle E, as if he were a celebrity. Everyone ate it up—this story of redemption.

"I think you will agree, brothers and sisters, that this young man holding back that gorgeous tenor from us for so long—*that's* the crime," the rev said.

Uncle E led us into the anthem "Lift Ev'ry Voice," and it was official: With his gift of pitch and smooth vocal flexibility, he was Dardon's own first man of song.

Afterwards, Mrs. Langley leaned over to me and complimented, "Your uncle is such a great singer. I wonder if he could win a contest."

"I don't know about that," I said. "But he for sure could win an *ex-con*test."

That earned Ma's frown.

We all moved downstairs for more celebration. We had red punch and cake, yellow on the inside and chocolate on the outside. That left me with mixed emotions. Did one have to go to jail to get a standing O? Or was all this about their discovery of his vast musical talents? What would their reaction to me be if I came back from the big house inhaling and exhaling into a tuba?

Uncle E even had a few ladies talking to him that day. Idabelle Ellis, with her big Hershey Bar–colored eyes. Clara Boyle, who worked for Bell Telephone Company and lived with her widowed father. And Bernice Jones, with her swaying walk.

This movie was writing itself right before my eyes. I knew exactly where he was headed. Picnics in the park. Long strolls on Penn's Landing. Maybe even marital bliss.

Well, at least he'd be happy from now on.

twenty-seven

Spring raking was different from autumn raking. Live things like worms, both pink and slate gray, crawled around. The dirt was rich and black, not brown. The shaggy, soft grass had yield to it.

I had come out to tell Tracy John and Leo that supper was in fifteen minutes. Before I was able to, out of the corner of my eye, I saw my skinny ex-paramour, wearing a grin wider than a crocodile's, sandwiched between my best friends Millicent and Cissy. All parties had their heads back, laughing. Their coats were open because, after all, it was late March.

Millicent lived on Orchard Avenue and Cissy's house was way past Church Lane. Since when did they ever come this way unless they were coming to see me? They ambled on down Dardon Avenue, not even bothering to look toward my house. My eyes strained at this sight; my breathing became shorter and shallower until I felt myself surrendering to the ground. My legs kicked out, and I heard someone scream "Maine!" but it was too late. I was down for the count.

Seconds before my eyes opened and my senses were gathered, I lingered in this state of unconsciousness. Then all of a sudden, I got drenched.

"I'll get another bucket to dump on her," I heard Tracy John say.

I opened my eyes and held out both hands. "Wait, I'm up. I'm up."

Ma had come out and she, Tracy John, and Leo formed a small circle around me. Leo pulled me up to my feet, and they all rushed me inside and laid me down on the living room sofa and fanned me. I was there into the evening.

Time wore on, and I edged out of my soupiness: brain waves fine, oxygen flow okey-dokey. No sooner had I gotten to my feet than Leo's voice rang out. "Charmaine's up!"

"And walking!" Tracy John shouted.

"It's a miracle!" Leo hollered.

"All right, boys." Daddy, who was right behind them, cleared them away. "Give her space to breathe.

"What brought this on?" Daddy pressed. "What happened?"

I couldn't tell Daddy about what had really caused my spell.

"Maybe she has high blood pressure," Tracy John supposed aloud, once again the junior MD.

"I think she was frightened by a trash can," Leo suggested, snickering.

What compassion, what sensitivity.

"This is not a laughing matter, Leo," Daddy said gravely.

"I feel better now," I said.

Daddy braced my shoulders. "Now, just stay still. Stay still and rest."

The next day, Daddy kept me home from school for monitoring. The extra hours in bed made my Afro mash down almost beyond recognition. I was combing it out around four when my visitors arrived.

"Cissy and Millicent are here to see you," Tracy John told me.

"I don't want to talk to them." I waved my hand. "Please tell them to leave."

From the hallway, I heard him ignoring my request. "Come right this way," he said.

When Millicent and Cissy entered the room, I couldn't even look in their direction. I could feel their eyes crawling on me.

"You look fine," Cissy said.

"I'm not fine. I'm under observation."

"Psychiatric?" Millicent asked.

I gave a fake laugh.

"When are you coming back to school?" Millicent asked.

I turned to them. "What difference does that make to you?"

"I guess eight years of friendship means nothing to you," Cissy answered.

"You've got the whole thing backwards, Cissy. My friendship means nothing to either of you," I said.

"Your friendship meant a lot to us. You're the one who never has any time for us," Cissy said.

"That's not true. I always asked you along. You always said no."

"We didn't want to be—" Millicent began.

"And don't start that third-wheel business. I have never tried to exclude you. And if that wasn't bad enough, I saw you with Raymond."

"So?" Millicent asked.

"You aren't going to try to deny that?"

"Why should we?" Cissy asked.

"So you admit you are going out with him?"

"How could both of us be going out with him?" Cissy asked.

"Yeah, and besides, we would never go out with someone you used to go out with."

"Then what were you doing with him? And walking in front of my house, no less."

"Do you own Dardon Avenue?" Millicent asked.

"Yeah, Maine, you sound really paranoid. There was a truck blocking Church Lane, that's why we were on 'your' street. But yes, we did go over Raymond's house the other day," Cissy said.

"Aha!" I not only sprang up, but I pointed.

"But all we did was look at Hollywood books," Millicent said.

"Is that some kind of code?"

Millicent rolled her eyes. "You've got everything all wrong. All he ever talks about is you; Raymond is hope-lessly taken by you."

"And we didn't stop spending time with you. You stopped spending time with us," Cissy said once again.

They both turned and stomped out. No sooner were they gone than Leo's head appeared at the doorjamb.

"That went well," he said.

I threw a pillow at him. Of course, I missed.

twenty-eight

Time expands and contracts, even in sleep. Before dawn, I had the strangest dream. I somehow felt as if I were in a bed of small snakes. They felt like slime. They slithered all over my limbs and torso, and they were trying to get to my face, up my nose, and in my ears, but I kept vigilant. I swatted wildly. It was a battle royal, with me twisting and turning.

And then I woke up and saw Tracy John dangling a worm over me.

I screamed, and he took off running. I put on my robe and chased after him, but by the time I got downstairs, he was already outside by Daddy's station wagon.

He waved at me, and I shook my fist at him. Then he leaned over to Leo, who was standing by the car, no doubt telling him what he'd done. Soon both heads were bobbing with laughter. Daddy and Uncle E were steadily loading up the car.

I snapped my fingers. That was right, this was the day they were supposed to go fishing.

I marched back into the house, passing Ma, who was carrying brown paper bags.

"Here are the sandwiches. I put in a plain cheese sandwich for Raymond," she said.

I spun around. "Raymond?" I made a beeline for Tracy John. "Is Raymond going with you?"

"Well, he couldn't invite him and then not invite him," Leo said.

"Yeah, that would be rude," Tracy John said.

"I hope he gets bitten by a bear!" I told them.

Ma drew back in horror. "What a horrible thing to say!"

"I mean it. As the old folks say, I solid mean it," I said, and stormed back into the house.

After she came back in, Ma *tsk-tsk*ed me. She told me I was being pigheaded and that I should get over myself and make up with that "well-mannered young man." I rolled my eyes. She was a fine one to come chiming in at this late date like she was some kind of expert in male-female dynamics! Sure, she had been happily married for eighteen years and everything, but she didn't have to go on and on like she was sitting atop a high mountain.

She handed me the duster. She told me to go down the banister but to be sure to stop if I felt woozy.

"I slept the day away yesterday, Ma. I'm not going to drop," I reassured her.

"Well, go ahead then, make yourself useful, Charmaine."

After I completed that task, Ma and I cleaned the windows in silence. I next vacuumed the carpets, which totally erased the quiet, as she swept the front stoop. We finished all those tasks by noon. Instead of sitting down, Ma snapped her apron in the air. She said it never hurt to get a head start on tomorrow's cooking, it being Sunday and all. As she began battering okra (like anyone had a fondness for that vegetable, breaded or otherwise), I took the opportunity to slip out.

I went to the living room and turned on the TV. Usually on Saturday, there were wall-to-wall sports shows on the major network channels and creature double features on UHF. Somehow, on channel forty-eight, I happened onto a movie called *Algiers*, starring Hedy Lamarr. I remembered her from the Hollywood book. She was hailed as the "most fabulous brunette ever" and was called a term that I hadn't seen before: "a Jewess." Originally from Austria, she slipped out of Europe just before the Nazis came to power. With that dramatic background, I expected to see real acting from her. What she delivered instead was presence. Her expression was still and singular, yet this repose transmitted volumes.

The plot of *Algiers* was allegorical. Hedy's character was a social climber who married well, in the financial sense only. From their first scene together, it was clear that she had no love for her new husband, who was twice her age and size. Soon she met a romantic jewel thief, played by Charles Boyer, who, the Hollywood book claimed, was fluent in French, Spanish, German, and Italian, but from listening to him, he was severely limited in English. Most actors like him were bumped from talkies, but actually his heavy accent aided his delivery of the immortal line: "Come with me to the casbah."

Even though I didn't know what a casbah was, I was hooked. I was so wrapped in the story that it didn't dawn on me till the flick's end that though they were in North Africa, all the natives were kept to the background.

Besides any sense of political consciousness, my principles also went out the window. I really hoped that the affair between this kept woman and a crook would work out. It was all romance, romance, romance. It convinced you that you were really having an experience, while in reality you were just sitting there watching a box. That's Hollywood.

Around nine that night, they came in smelling of the great outdoors. Uncle E carried Tracy John straight up to bed.

"One day in the country plumb tired him out," Daddy explained as he carried a container into the kitchen.

Though I didn't like fish (they are so weird—they look oily, but they feel dry), I followed him in for a peek.

They certainly had a wide array: butterfish, porgies, flukes, and a few crappies.

"This one looks good," I said, pointing.

"That's Raymond's catch," Leo told me.

I frowned. I should have known. I made a mental note to myself not to eat any of his crappies.

How was it possible to dislike and like someone with the same intensity? Not long before, I'd believed we would always be together. What could go wrong? We seemed to have so very much in common. In truth, we were in two different places. Better that I learned that now rather than later. Just think if we ever got married. I'd have to cook two different meals for dinner each night. One normal. One without meat. And we'd have two different locales to be on Sunday. He'd have Latin Mass, and I would have Reverend Clee.

My brother told me, "Raymond really likes you, Maine."

I sensed that I was being set up. "What's the punch line, Leo?"

He shrugged and said, "There is none."

twenty-nine

"He lost his canoe, his house, his son," Mr. Mand said.

"And his dignity," Raymond added.

"It seems like the author is trying to show us that money is the root of all evil," Mr. Mand said.

Raymond nodded. "It turned him into a gangster."

That's how English class went on Monday morning, just the two of them dialoguing. Two yes-men agreeing with each other, paying homage to the vision of a classless society. I watched the clock's second hand move so slowly, I couldn't take forty more minutes of this. I had to jump in.

"Maybe the author's trying to say that the lack of money's the root, not the money itself," I replied to Raymond without looking at him. "I mean, at least he made an attempt. Besides belting his wife, everything Kino did was to make a better life for his family. He wanted his son to have an education. He wanted to marry his wife formally in the church, and that takes money."

"He forgot about his loved ones," Raymond said. "All he cared about was the pesos he was going to get. After the pearl went to his head, he went bananas. He lost his simpleness."

"Since when is simpleness the same as goodness?" I asked. I held up the book. "That's where Steinbeck goes off the deep end. Just because Kino wants things doesn't make him a bad person."

Raymond's eyes remained forward, not looking at me. "He's not so much a bad person as a blind person."

"Everyone has a blind spot, Raymond."

Behind me, I felt the class pulse alive.

"You can say that again." Raymond's voice went up a decibel. "Some people don't know how to leave well enough alone."

"Maybe that's why you took up with my two best friends," I blurted out.

"What page are they on?" I heard someone behind me ask.

I continued my attack. I faced Raymond and offered incontestable evidence. "I saw you. I saw you! You were on my street. You don't have to go past Dardon Avenue to get to Redwood Avenue. You wanted me to catch you."

Intrigued, Mr. Mand looked over the top of his glasses at us.

The class went "Ohhhhhhhh."

"I'm not going out with Cissy or Millicent," Raymond said.

"You expect me to believe that?" I asked.

"You can believe whatever you want, Maine. I'm telling you the truth." He shook his head gravely and pointed at me. "You threw away your pearl."

Now the class was absolutely still. Out of the corner of my eye, I saw a smile hovering on Dinah's lips. Demetrius looked equally amused.

"You call yourself a pearl? Of all the arrogance! Of all the gall!" I continued my outburst, in spite of my better judgment. I was positively on fire.

"This book is better than I thought," someone from the back row said.

"I'm not the pearl, Maine," Raymond said. "Our feelings for one another, that's the pearl."

For a second or two, I felt like Neil Armstrong, you know, the first man on the moon. It was such a revelation knowing that Raymond felt that deeply.

"Oh," I said after a long lapse of time.

Mr. Mand's mouth, usually a hard line, was now open and animated. He was truly caught up in this junior high soap opera. Suddenly I was not just the smart girl. I was a fool, a romantic fool, but a fool nonetheless. I was not sure I wanted my English teacher to see me in this light. What if I needed a recommendation for something?

Mr. Mand said, "I thank you, Raymond and Charmaine, for your input. It's important to feel what you read. To get inside the words and make them relevant to your life."

161

He went on that way for another few moments; then he read the concluding pages of *The Pearl*. At last the ordeal was over.

The buzzer sounded and we were free to go our separate ways.

Hot with embarrassment, I prayed for the floor to swallow me up as I made my way from Mr. Mand's classroom, not daring to look back. When you're five-foot-eight in the ninth grade, you have no choice but to walk tall. No amount of slouching was going to make me invisible, so I threw my shoulders back.

From third period the day wore on. You know what they say: Time heals and flies. But it did neither that day. I don't know how celebrities stood it, with all their business thrown out on Front Street.

In the lunch line, I felt hands on my shoulders. "We heard," they said. It was Cissy and Millicent. We sat at our usual spot, and they commiserated with me.

There's some saying that the only thing worse than being talked about is not being talked about.

I disagree with that statement.

Outside, the sun was shining and the birds were singing, but inside, I'd managed to wreck everything again.

I deposited my books in my locker at the end of the day to lighten my load. No Monday homework, just a light reading assignment for history.

"Maine," someone said. My heart leapt because there was no mistaking his voice. At the sight of his tiny, cramped shoulders and broad smiling face, I thought I might melt.

"I was wondering if you might like to go for a soda or something."

All the phrases I had prepared for this moment dissolved at once, like a bubble of foam.

"Tracy John has a game . . . ," I began.

"Oh," he said, crestfallen.

"I don't mean it like that. You're more than welcome to join me." I rushed to say, "I—I mean, I'd like you to. Raymond, I'm so sorry. I don't know how I could have made you feel like I didn't care about you, because nothing, *nothing* could be farther from the truth."

"No, Maine, I'm sorry. I did overreact to things and blow them all out of proportion."

I held out my arms and said a really cliché line: "Oh, Raymond, let's never quarrel again."

We embraced.

Off to the side, Cissy and Millicent both gave us the thumbs-up.

thirty

America has only come up with three originals: jazz music, comic books, and baseball. Though many more pastimes have woven their way into our country's lore, baseball is king.

Raymond and I held hands as we made our way to the bleachers.

Tracy John rushed up to us. "I didn't know you'd be here, Raymond."

I was in shock. "So now you know his name."

Raymond tugged on his cap. "Tracy John can call me whatever he wants."

Happy to have that door open, my cousin looked at me with eyes that sparkled at the prospect of mischief.

Raymond and Tracy John did a two-minute handshake like long-lost soul brothers.

"Is Spider-Man your boyfriend again?" Tracy John asked me.

My "I hope so" ran into Raymond's "Of course I am."

"Good, cuz Maine's not so bad," he told Raymond.

"Thank you, Tracy John."

"You have to get used to her."

My grin turned tight. "Thank you, Tracy John," I repeated.

"Because," he continued, "she thinks she knows everything."

"Thank you."

"I mean she can be bossy."

Was there no stopping him? "Thank you, Tracy—"

"—But she's getting better." He finished his point with his eyes wide. As my reflection filled his irises, I couldn't help but cave and give his terminally adorable face a big kiss.

After Tracy John returned to the field, Raymond asked me, "Hey, can I have one of those?"

I removed my glasses and closed my eyes. I certainly didn't need twenty-twenty vision for this. Our lips met, and it felt like the first time: majestic and timeless, warm and surprising.

"Hey, you never told me, Maine, how did that modeling contest work out?"

I chuckled a little. "Not so well. It wasn't what I expected. Thanks for entering me, though."

He shook his head mournfully. "Their loss."

I realized that as far as the four fs of life were concerned, I was right back where I'd started. No fame. No fortune. All I had were family and friends. And deep down, I guess I always knew that was the better part of the bargain.

The umpire raised the flag while we sang the national anthem. Then it was time to play ball. The sun ebbed bright through the trees. They said, "Batter up!" but I had to wait till late in the third inning for my cousin to take to the plate.

The pitcher, who was a third grader and could do curves, released the ball. It wound closer and closer to home plate, where Tracy John stood ready and able. His expression turned serious.

The chances swelled.

I moved to the edge of my seat, and Raymond squeezed my hand.

The moment before Tracy John's swing seemed so long, but I thought that very moment was perfect.

I wished it could have lasted forever.

ABOUT THE AUTHOR

A Philadelphia native and a Virgo, Allison Whittenberg studied dance for years before switching her focus to writing. She has an MA in English from the University of Wisconsin and enjoys traveling to places like the Caribbean and Russia. Her first novel about Charmaine and Tracy John, *Sweet Thang,* is available from Yearling Books. She is also the author of *Life Is Fine,* a novel for teenagers available from Delacorte Press.